CANNIBAL CREATOR

by

Chad Lutzke

To join my VIP reader list and be included in all future giveaways, visit www.chadlutzke.com
To become a patron and receive exclusive content, visit www.patreon.com/ChadLutzke

Introduction

I don't believe in guilty pleasures. We like what we like. Each of us have our own individuality, life experiences, and nostalgic triggers. There should be no shame found in that.

As a punk rock metalhead, I shouldn't feel guilty for cranking Madonna, Sade, or The Cure. As a diehard horror fan, I shouldn't feel guilty for enjoying romance films like *The Notebook*, or ugly crying during the season finale of *Six Feet Under* (if you didn't cry too, you're not human...or you're probably a cannibal). All that to say, I have no guilty pleasures.

Except one.

The Italian cannibal films from the 70s (and early 80s) probably should have never been made. Why? Because a native tribe murdering nonlocals to feast on their flesh isn't the only common denominator these films have. It's the butchering of innocent animals on film. We're not talking special effects here. These hold animal snuff segments, featuring disembowelment, dismemberment, bludgeoning, and

4

skinning, *Cannibal Holocaust* being the most notable, with the highest animal death count. But there's something about that movie I thoroughly enjoy, hence the guilt. It could be the survival horror aspect, the lush jungle locale, or my curious fascination with people who desire to eat their own. Or it could be the nostalgia. One thing I know for sure I'm drawn to is the lack of any supernatural element.

Except for a few short stories, maybe you've read enough of my books to find I tend to steer clear of anything supernatural. If I'm writing horror, I write what scares me. Ghouls and ghosts don't do that. But people do. And with the cannibal films, there's no single serial killer stalking its prey. This is a collective group of people with one goal in mind: To end your life (brutally) and eat your flesh.

While *Cannibal Creator* is my homage to those Italian cannibal films from the 70s and 80s, don't expect a retelling. This isn't Eli Roth and *Green Inferno*. I didn't set out to plant people in an isolated jungle just to kill them. Maybe that's what you wanted. It can be fun to spend 90 minutes watching a rehash. But with books, there's a much longer investment, so you may as well get something different.

The jungle, the killing, the eating, the savages. It's all here. But with *Cannibal Creator*, I wanted to fuse the familiar with the unchartered. A twist on an old story if you will.

That being said, do be warned, people eating people isn't the only common denominator here. While no real animals were harmed in the writing of this story, some pretend ones were.

~Chad

"Won't go to bed hungry. No, not tonight."

~ Starved to Death, The Accused

Chapter 1

Buulato Island, 1980

Simon Lanovich wore his lab coat with pride. He brushed a spot of dirt from it and pulled a pen from the pocket.

Wearing the heavily bleached garment was unnecessary—which Dr. Barnard stated often—but it made him feel more like a scientist than a monster who'd been hermitized. His only personal complaint being that it dirtied quickly, particularly on feeding day. Today.

"You awake?" he asked the man who slept on a lumpy mattress in the far side of a makeshift cell built from thick sheets of plywood and two-by-fours. The walls were covered in stick-figure graffiti drawn in crayon—depictions of what Simon assumed were the family members of those who'd spent time in the room, though what he found most interesting was the many drawings of the sun, long rays stretching far across the wooden canvas, as though the cell's inhabitants desired it most—to be standing within its optimistic glow, casting hope upon them.

But he couldn't dwell on such things, approaching work while facing a moral dilemma, because this was science, and science didn't allow for that. A Conscience. Empathy. And worst of all, guilt. There was an endgame here. The outcome was knowledge, and getting there was a road paved with tortured creatures—probed brains and singed flesh. Broken limbs and exposed ribs. Every bit of it for a reason. Dr. Barnard had promised.

"Are you awake?" he asked again.

The man didn't move. Perfect.

Simon stuck a key in the door and turned it. The latch bolt freed and seemed to echo in the eight-by-eight box. Heavily drugged, the man still didn't stir. Simon approached him and continued with the usual routine of restraining the prey and covering its head with a canvas bag.

Simon rushed through the dense jungle with a wheelbarrow on a well-beaten path. He wore protective gear now, his lab coat buried under a padded suit, while his thick rubber gloves and leather boots covered his hands and feet. Over his head was a visorless motorcycle helmet—all of his gear painted or dyed green to match the foliage. He carried a pistol strapped to his side, though in twenty years has never had to use it.

After nearly a mile, he slowed, then stopped at a clearing where a large flat rock sat in the center. The rock's surface was stained with the blood of countless offerings. All in the name of science. The word had become his mantra, particularly in moments like this.

Simon spilled his cargo from the wheelbarrow. The man groaned but didn't move. If this were a child, or even a fragile woman, Simon would turn them loose in the jungle, letting the tribe revel in the thrill of the hunt. But an unrestrained grown man could prove harmful to the project, potentially risking the life of tribe members, which had nearly happened once before.

Before he allowed himself any internal struggle with a moral dilemma, he pulled a machete from his side and brought it down, severing the man's head from his body with a wet thwack. A quiet sigh escaped the open trachea, forming a crimson bubble that covered the new hole.

He then quickly dismembered the arms and legs and stacked them on the rock. The torso he left on the ground. He'd watched the tribe enough to know they preferred it this way, treating the rest of the body as luggage that stored the vital organs which were not eaten but used for rope and waterskins.

Simon looked away from the gore. He hated dismembering. That part didn't feel like science at all. It felt like gloating, even if the subjects felt nothing.

Subjects.

Martyrs in the name of science.

Simon ran with the wheelbarrow back toward the compound. Once he cleared the first curve in the path, he stopped and buried himself within the camouflaging jungle, watching. Waiting for them to come, and receive.

Hours went by before two children appeared at the rock. Two children dressed in rags that covered their genitals, though shirtless. Hair in nappy dreads. The boy wore his dreads long, much longer than the girl. His skin was brown, the girl's pale. The two studied the surrounding foliage, looking for any sign of the one who delivered, then gave up only a moment later. The girl loaded the boy's arms with two of the severed limbs, as if they were logs for a nearby campfire. They would be back for the rest, or tell the others, and more would come, like bees that danced in their hive, giving directions.

Simon ungloved his hand and wiped sweat from his nose, then looked to his left. Hidden within the trees, some twenty yards away was a woman, watching him. Filled with shame, he nodded, assuming the gesture meant nothing to her.

Before the children walked away, heading into the dense jungle, the boy—with his arms full of murder—studied the area once more and said, "Thank you, God."

Chapter 2

Miami International Airport, Florida, 1980

Kevin Hummel closed a finger in the book he was reading and looked across the airport, watching for the Robertsons.

"They should have been here by now," he said to his wife. "This is just like Ross. Everything he does is last minute. When we've got a deadline approaching, he's up all night finishing the draft. How can you live like that? The stress would kill me."

"You need to calm down, Hummel. If you're going to be working your entire vacation, the least you can do is relax before it starts. Now, get back to reading. If they're not here in the next ten minutes, I'll call Jen."

With a headful of wavy gold and a body that easily forgave the birth of their son, Vicki Hummel was out of Kevin's league, if you didn't know him. Catching keepers was something he'd been doing since he was a freshman in high school, back when he went out with Samantha Brodock—a junior varsity cheerleader who forever falsely claimed her dad would never let her date. Until Kevin came along. Call it charisma or the chiseled jaw—it certainly wasn't his thinning hair—grabbing the attention of a beautiful woman was something he was good at, like tennis and cooking. And writing.

He gave one more look around the airport, saw a man with a mohawk, wearing combat boots and a leather jacket. Kevin elbowed his 9-year-old son Caleb, who sat next to him, reading a comic book filled with ghostly tales. "How'd you like to have to walk around like that all day?"

The boy looked up and trailed his dad's line of vision. He laughed. "How do you even do that?"

"Hairspray, I suppose. Hell, maybe glue. Lookin' like that, he's probably sniffing it too."

Caleb offered a weak chuckle, as though he didn't get the joke.

Reading the comic over Caleb's shoulder was their nanny, Carmen. She'd helped raise the boy since day one. The Hummels were responsible for helping her become a US citizen after she moved to Florida from

Venezuela. Like a member of the family, Carmen lived at the house, using the finished attic as an apartment. When she wasn't taking care of the boy, cooking, or cleaning, she spent her time with photography, her apartment walls covered in moody black and whites, two of which she'd won an award for.

Reacquainting herself with the Caribbean, as well as the chance at shooting pictures of the familiar sea, the trip to Barbados had her more excited than any of them.

"De miedo," Carmen said in Caleb's ear.

The boy laughed. "It's not scary."

She smiled and gave a teasing nod.

"*Jaws* is scary."

"You see Jaws?" Carmen asked, then frowned. She slapped Kevin on his back. "You let boy see shark movie?"

Kevin flinched, then turned. "What...he's old enough."

"Carmen's right," Vicki said, then lowered her voice so only her husband could hear. "And horrible timing, Kevin. You expect him to swim in the ocean now?"

"It's a PG movie."

"That's not the point. I don't want him scared to swim his whole life, especially right now."

"That's ridiculous. You coddle him too much. Hell, I'm surprised you allow him to read those comics."

"I don't coddle him. I mother him. And you're supposed to father him, which means keeping him away from things that could scar him."

Kevin looked around, made sure Carmen and Caleb weren't listening, then lowered his voice even more. "What...you think by watching a horror movie he's tainted somehow? Like he'll never be normal? Listen to yourself, Vicki."

She rolled her eyes. "No, I don't think he's *tainted*. But I think the human psyche can only take so much."

"How many horror movies do you think you've seen? How many of those books have you read? King and Poe and what's her name. The woman who wrote—"

"Shirley Jackson?"

"Right...how much of that have you ingested?"

Vicki kept quiet.

"Yet you sleep just fine, you're not hiding under the covers, or running around with a knife, or worshipping the de—"

"That's different. He's just a boy. His mind is still growing. He's impressionable."

"You know...you've done this kind of shit his whole life. Treated me like I'm a useless, inadequate father, completely incapable of teaching him anything or being a role model."

Vicki looked over at Carmen, who was busy keeping Caleb's attention. Looked back at Kevin. "Now who's being ridiculous?"

"I'll be sure and check with you before we watch another movie, since I'm not capable of making wise decisions regarding our son's wellbeing."

"Just stop filling his head with—"

"It's a fucking movie, Vicki. A PG movie."

Vicki shook her head and looked away. The conversation was done now. Kevin peeked at what his son was reading and saw comic panels filled with skeletal figures and shrieking women. He looked up, and Carmen was staring at him. She winked and smiled, sultry like. He threw his eyes back on the comic, wondering if this whole vacation was a mistake. He could have stayed here in Miami and written the book with Ross, rented a place like they did with the first book in the series, just the two of them and a case of brandy. No distractions.

"You're not scared of the water are you, Caleb?" he asked his son.

Caleb rolled his eyes and laughed. "No way. Plus, Carmen said there aren't any sharks in Barbados and that even if there were, the water is so clear you could see them a mile away."

Kevin mussed his son's hair and smiled. When he looked up, Carmen was eyeing him again. His smile faded, but hers lingered. He'd made a huge mistake.

Chapter 3

Robertson residence, Miami, Florida

Ross Robertson was on the portly side. He blamed his wife's cooking for that, though she would remind him if she can keep the weight off, he could too. Nearly in their forties now, the weight loss gripe became more frequent, though never out of malice. She was legitimately concerned for his health. *"If you don't keep tabs on it now, by the time you're fifty you'll have to lose a pound for each year. I don't want to see you drop dead of a heart attack."*

He ran to the taxicab parked in front of his house, arms full of luggage. "Jen? What time is it?"

Jennifer Robertson had a suitcase in one hand and their 8-year-old daughter's hand in the other. "I don't know, but if you're wondering if we're late, we are."

Ross nodded at the cab driver who had opened the trunk, then stacked the luggage inside. "For the flight? Or to meet Kevin and Vicki?"

"We'll make the flight." Jennifer caught up and added her suitcase to the rest of them, while their daughter hopped in the back of the cab. "Melanie?"

"I'm in the car, Mom."

"Did you get Foozoo?"

"He's in my lap...the seats are hot." Melanie smoothed out her dress, then bounced the plush ape on her legs and stuck its hard-plastic thumb in its open mouth.

"We'll be out of the cab in ten minutes, honey," her father said.

"Uhh, sir," the cabdriver said. "Traffic is pretty congested right now, and you *are* going to the airport."

"Twenty minutes, honey. Tops"

The trunk closed and the family piled in. As they pulled away from the house, Melanie waved goodbye to it, then squeezed Foozoo tight.

Jennifer opened her purse and pulled out a small notepad.

"I don't want to hear the checklist, Jen. If we forgot something, we'll just have to deal with it. No turning back now."

"I just wanted to make sure we at least had the essentials."

"We *are* the essentials. That's all we need."

Jennifer leaned back in surprise. "That's pretty maudlin, even for you."

"Hey...no big words while my thesaurus is packed."

"And you call yourself a writer." Jennifer faced her daughter, patted her on the knee. "You excited to see Caleb?"

"I guess so."

"You two had fun last time. Remember the lake? You collected all that pretty driftwood."

"It'd be better if he was a girl."

"Fair enough." Jennifer turned back to her husband. "Speaking of boys, you two had better not hide away the entire week."

"Well, it is the reason for the trip in the first place, Jen."

"Don't you dare. If we're going to the Caribbean, you're going to have to split your time. I want the camera loaded with pictures of us together."

Ross put his arm around his wife and kissed her on the cheek. "Don't worry, we'll make plenty of memories. Besides, I can only take so much of Kevin. He gets a little alpha when it comes to collaborating."

"You mean he's passionate about what he writes."

"I guess you could call it that."

"What's alpha mean?" Melanie asked.

Jennifer leaned over and whispered in her husband's ear. "You'd better start watching what you say about your partner, this one's taking notes."

Chapter 4

It was nearly a three-hour flight to San Juan. Kevin and Ross sat together, already brainstorming, while their wives were seated in front of them, going over their own plans for Barbados. Caleb and Melanie sat directly across the aisle, reading a comic together while discussing which superpower they'd want if given the choice. Caleb chose invisibility, because he could sneak around and play pranks, like make fart noises in class. Melanie favored flying. *"I could make friends with the birds, and we could fly over the rooftops."*

Next to them, taking the aisle seat, was Carmen, sitting quietly and periodically dozing.

Drinks were ordered but food was not. They'd agreed to wait until arriving in San Juan and have something local. Cigarette smoke from the passengers behind him stung Kevin's eyes, and more than once he shot them a glance, hoping they'd catch on—Just because you can smoke in the closed space doesn't mean you have to. If they were in front of him, he'd *accidentally* kick the seat whenever they lit up.

"If this is the final book in the series, we'll need more closure than that," Ross said, stirring his gin and tonic with a toothpick.

"I don't think there's anything wrong with ambiguity. It leaves the reader with something to consider, to make their own mind up about what happens. I don't want to spell it out for them."

"It's not spelling it out. It's closure."

"We don't want closure. We want the story to linger, to never leave their mind. Let's give the reader just enough to make a judgment call that's more than likely accurate."

Ross seemed to consider it. "You know we're gonna get some readers who absolutely hate that."

"Let 'em. There'll be more who appreciate not being spoon-fed."

Ross sighed. "Okay. But let it be known, I'm washing my hands of any critic's blood. That'll be on you."

Vicki sipped on her bloody Mary after complaining about the taste for the third time, comparing it to the one she had at a Christmas party three years ago, deeming that one the best she'd ever have, and if she could, she'd hire the bartender to work for her every night.

Jennifer made no comment about the drink, other than the celery being unnecessary, and steered the conversation back to their vacation. "Even if all they do is hole up somewhere and write their book, at least we'll have the beach."

"And the lifeguards," Vicki joked.

Jennifer looked over at the kids, at Carmen, who had her eyes closed. "You're blessed to have her, ya know. She's so good with Caleb."

"She has been helpful." Vicki lowered her voice to a whisper. "But I'm thinking of letting her go."

Jennifer gasped. "Really? But she's been with you for nine years. And between your work and Kevin's, I'd think you'd still need her."

"We need *someone*. But I think she's...overstayed her welcome."

25

Jennifer couldn't help but look back at Carmen with sympathetic eyes before responding. "What do you mean?"

"I just think it's time for her to move on, maybe get a career. She's nearly thirty, you know. I wouldn't want to hold her back."

"I'd assume if that's what she wanted she would have done that on her own."

"Or she feels obligated to stick around for Caleb. If I let her go, it'll spare her the guilt."

"I suppose. But maybe you should give her the option."

"We'll see." Vicki took a sip of her drink and scrunched her face. "I think it's the salt. There's too much."

Jennifer drank hers, shrugged, then looked back at Carmen again, who was now awake, with her eyes on Kevin.

Chapter 5

They were seated outside a restaurant called Rincon Criollo, eating food, most of which was suggested by Carmen. Ross, having never been to Puerto Rico, insisted she order the food for them. Halfway through the meal, they combined their orders, dipping into each other's plates like a buffet.

"Hey, Carmen…" Ross said through a mouthful of mofongo. "How do you say, 'where's the men's room' in Spanish?"

Carmen wiped her mouth on a napkin. "Dónde está el baño de hombres."

Ross fumbled through the words. "Donde esta…"

"El baño."

"El ban no."

"De hombres."

"Day umbrees." He gave a confident smile.

"Si."

Kevin stood up. "Speaking of restroom, don't mind if I do."

"Another drink, dear?" Vicki held her empty glass in the air.

Kevin, feeling uneasy about yet another request for alcohol from his wife, spoke as gently and undemanding as he could. "We've got another flight ahead of us, honey. How about we wait until—."

"That's exactly the point," she said. "I need something to calm my nerves. Charter planes don't feel safe. We should have just flown commercial." She turned her attention toward Jennifer. "Have you ever ridden in a charter plane?"

"I think it's a jet," Jennifer said.

"What's the difference?"

This turned into a back-and-forth discussion between the women regarding the questionable safety of such planes—or jets—so, Kevin took advantage of the distraction and slipped away to the restroom, with no intention of bringing his wife another drink.

This was the part of the vacation he wasn't looking forward to, his wife's affinity for alcohol and the embarrassment it sometimes brought in the presence of others. But nobody had ever said a word about it.

Instead, there seemed to be an unspoken understanding of the problem, that this was just how Vicki is. He could see it in their sympathetic eyes, except for Jennifer. She was clueless. But that's just who she was. Whether it was naivety or unconditional love for everyone around her, he wasn't sure. Most likely love. And empathy. She was an exceptionally caring and patient woman. Kevin didn't have half the marriage his co-author did. The couple never fought, never disagreed on whether or not they should let their kid watch PG movies. He never so much as got a whiff of passive aggressive signals between the two perfect pair. It was infuriating and hopeful at the same time.

As Kevin was relieving himself, the bathroom door swung open and in walked Carmen.

"Are you out of your mind?" Kevin said.

She looked down at his crotch. He turned away, splashing the side of the urinal.

"Let me see," she said with her thick accent, walking closer.

"Carmen, you need to get out of here, now."

"Let me touch." She stood close, put her arms around him and slid her hands down, searching for his penis.

Kevin pinched off and spun away, getting out of her grasp. Piss dribbled onto his khakis, darkening them. "Get the fuck out."

"Fine. But when we are in Barbados, you better—"

"Nothing is happening in Barbados, Carmen. What we did is never going to happen again."

Years ago, Carmen had developed an intense attraction to Kevin, something he suspected but never entertained, not until last week, during a drunken stupor after fighting with his wife about their disintegrating sex life. The quick moment with Carmen was nothing more than anger-fueled revenge that felt justified, particularly considering what Vicki had done to him more times than he cared to remember. But with Carmen, he was afraid he'd created a monster.

"I sorry, Kevin. I should not have come to you like this. I should have waited until safe. But please don't say never again. Please."

"Leave." Kevin put his back to her and stood up to the urinal, finishing.

"Don't be mad, please. I do not want that."

"Now. Please."

Carmen hung her head and slipped out of the restroom.

Kevin sensed his marriage would dissolve soon (*would that be so bad?*), his son would lose his stability, and if Carmen's risky visit to the men's room was any indication of just how unhealthy her infatuation was, that was a whole other mess he wasn't sure how to deal with.

Chapter 6

On unsteady feet, Vicki Hummel climbed into the jet. "Oh, I just don't know about this."

"We're fine, honey. Flying is safer than driving," Kevin held her hand until she was in completely.

"Not on these planes. I'll bet they go down more than you know. We just don't hear about it."

"You're perfectly safe, ma'am." A heavyset pilot sat in the front, strapped in, and sporting a headset. "I've flown this particular jet to and from Barbados hundreds of times. Only problem I've ever had was a pregnant woman about to deliver. And even then, we made it in time for her to have a healthy baby at San Juan Regional."

"Well, it's not quite as crowded as I pictured," she said.

Jennifer climbed in next, then the children, followed by Carmen. Kevin caught himself avoiding the sight of her, realizing he'd lost his poker face ever since her trip to the men's room. Last in was Ross. Kevin sat in front, next to the pilot. He wore a matching headset and struck up a conversation about how he'd always wanted to learn to fly.

Part of Kevin wanted to be sitting in the back, next to his wife, knowing she would be holding his hand tight, showing him affection he rarely got, even if it was superficial and based out of fear. Of course, some of his desire to sit with her was also created by guilt.

The hell do I have to feel guilty about? She had it coming.

Considering himself educated in Caribbean geography, Ross pointed to landmark islands and offered trivia as they passed them by, from their name to their culture. Most of his information was correct.

"Where's Barbados, Daddy?" Melanie asked, holding Foozoo up to the window so he could see the water below.

"We're not quite there yet. Give it another half hour and we should see it. It's a beautiful piece of land. Clear blue water, lush greenery. Just gorgeous."

"Have you been there before?" she asked.

"No, but I've seen a lot of pictures."

Jennifer furrowed a concerned brow at Vicki and put a hand on her knee. "Are you okay?"

Vicki had grown pale, her hands shook. "I knew I should have had another drink."

Jennifer took Vicki's hand in hers. "You'll be fine. Before you know it, we'll be on the beach with a book in our hand and the sound of our children's laughter."

Vicki tried to smile, then saw the terror in her husband's face.

Kevin turned toward the pilot, grabbed his arm. "Sir?"

The pilot gave a confused look, his mouth crooked as though one side had melted.

"Sir, are you okay?"

The man stared with empty eyes. Kevin could feel him searching for words he couldn't find. "Huh?" was all he mustered.

Oh shit.

"I think he's having a stroke," Kevin yelled toward the back of the plane.

34

"What!?" Vicki screamed with wide eyes.

"Sir?" Kevin looked at the controls, the man's fat white knuckles gripping them.

"Oh God...I knew it. I just knew it," Vicki cried.

"What's a stroke?" Melanie's question went ignored.

Ross rushed the front of the jet. "Hey!" he shouted at the pilot, but the man kept his eyes on Kevin, as though in a trance.

"I d...don't...c...c...can't." The man finally tore his eyes from Kevin and darted them about slowly, from the controls to his legs, to the sky. It was clear he had no idea where he was or what he was doing.

"You gotta be kidding me," Ross said.

The jet began to descend.

"Do you know anything about flying?" Kevin asked Ross.

"Just pulling that control back and forth, the same shit we've all seen in movies."

The two studied the controls, trying to make sense of them.

"Mom, what's a stroke?"

"Dad…" Caleb got up, moved toward the front of the jet. "Are we gonna be okay?"

Vicki screamed. "Kevin! Do something!"

Jennifer grabbed Melanie and held her, speaking into her ear how much she loved her and that she was an angel sent from God and that the last eight years have been the best of her life because she was in them.

Kevin yelled at his son to sit down and buckle up.

The inside of the jet was filled with a cacophony of panicked voices as they descended lower still, heading toward an island that was absolutely not Barbados or any other Ross had identified.

The pilot's eyes closed, and his head bobbled. Kevin reached over him, hit a switch. The engine died.

Ross turned to his family. "We turned the engine off to slow us down. There's an island ahead. We're going to try and land on the shore. Just hold tight. As tight as you can."

Caleb buckled in.

Kevin pulled back the controls and felt the cold hands of the pilot. Whether it be his own doing or pure coincidence, the jet seemed to level out as it approached the island, giving him a small amount of optimism that they weren't about to die. He thought of crash landings in movies, hoping there was some truth to survivors walking away with only minor scrapes and bumps to the head.

Are you really going to invest your hope in what happens in the movies? We're all screwed. This is the end. No finished book, no grandkids, and the last sexual encounter you had was a vengeful fuck and not with the woman you married. Maybe you deserve to die.

With an arm wrapped around her son, Vicki screamed at Kevin to look at her, to look into her eyes. "I'm sorry, Kevin. I'm so sorry."

Kevin closed his eyes and screamed in absolute horror.

Carmen shouted. "I love you, Kevin! I've always loved you!"

Chapter 7

Though his head pounded from the impact, Kevin never lost consciousness. He didn't dare open his eyes. And which was worse, the echo of screams from only moments ago? Or when they abruptly stopped?

He listened for any movement. There was only the sound of the jungle—exotic birds he'd only ever heard in films. Finally, something shifted in the jet. A grunt, followed by heavy breathing that bordered on hyperventilation. It was Melanie. He was sure of it.

He wiggled his toes, stretched his arms, reached out to feel around him but would not open his eyes. Not yet. If he saw his family in pieces, it would kill him. He'd never recover, wandering the island with a broken heart and no reason to live. Even if a rescue party found him, he would stay and punish himself by eating the dung of the creatures he now lived among, praying a parasite would eat him from the inside out, or an enormous snake would crush him, ending his miserable life.

His hand hit skin. It was warm, smooth, hairless. None of the women were sitting up front when they crashed. This person shouldn't be here. Everyone but himself, the pilot, and perhaps Ross (he couldn't remember) should be in the back, belted in. Was the leg by itself? Severed from who it once belonged to?

Still refusing to look, he ran his fingers along the skin. There was no doubt it was a leg. A woman's leg. Kevin tried to recall what each of them were wearing. He remembered Melanie wearing a dress because her mother reminded her at least a few times to close her legs so no one could see her underpants, Jennifer eventually demonstrating with her own sundress how a lady should sit. But the leg was too thick to be Melanie's. This was not her.

Vicki rarely wore dresses. Business suits were her go-to for any occasion.

Carmen. He was ashamed to admit he knew exactly what she had worn—a white sundress that stopped just above the knee, with a pair of sandals, hair in a ponytail up high on her head, and earrings that would have looked too gaudy on anyone else.

The leg was Carmen's.

He stopped touching it, staving any guilt from the thought that if someone had to die—just one of them—he wished for it to be her.

He opened his eyes.

The first thing he saw was beyond the leg. The pilot. The man appeared intact, and Kevin wondered if the stroke hadn't killed him perhaps he may have lived. Then he saw Carmen. She'd been tossed forward between the seats and now rested on the control panel with her neck impossibly bent, eyes locked on him, legs open, exposing her satin panties, as though still inviting him in, even after death.

Her jaw rested broken on her neck, with several bottom teeth missing. He could only assume the throttle lever caught her on the way up.

Why wasn't she buckled in? Was she running toward the cockpit after him? Hoping to die in his arms? She had called out to him just before the crash, hadn't she?

He removed his shirt and covered her face. He couldn't let Caleb see her like this.

If Caleb was alive.

Ross lay face down on the floor between the seats, a small puddle of blood next to his head. Kevin placed a hand on his friend's back. He was breathing.

Kevin looked toward the back of the jet. Seats filled with slouching bodies, all of them buckled. No sign of blood or protruding bone, not from where he stood. But that meant nothing. The impact could have snapped necks or bitten off tongues, where they'd swallow them and choke. Death was filled with the unpredictable and the unforeseen.

Melanie was indeed the one breathing heavy. Her face was pale, her eyes rolling. She's in shock, Kevin thought. She'll be fine for now. He checked Caleb first. His son was alive. Kevin caressed his head, kissed him, and the boy shot his eyes open and screamed. He saw Carmen's legs.

"Carmen!"

Melanie's eyes rolled back, and she let her head fall against the seat, passing out.

"Carmen, help me. I'm stuck!" Caleb stretched his arms out as far as he could, reaching for Carmen.

It was in that moment Kevin realized a void in Caleb's life was being filled not by his mother or father but by a woman from Venezuela they hired two months after he was born. Carmen had been his mother, his father, his best friend, his playmate. With Kevin busy writing and Vicki always at the office, their paychecks made it easy to have their son taken care of. But the one thing he needed most was something money could never buy. Kevin had failed.

He recalled the discussion he'd had with Vicki regarding the need for a nanny. Initially, he'd been adamant about Vicki quitting her job so she could be at home. "I make plenty to support us," he'd said. Early on, he knew the child needed his mother, not some stranger. But Vicki was no housewife. She had her own master's degree, worked very hard for it. It wasn't in her blood to only be a mother and a wife. She needed more. So, she'd made the convincing argument that the more money they made, the more they could provide for their child, and the more he would have. Her words seemed to wipe away any logic Kevin once held, like some spell cast upon him.

And until the moment he saw his horrified son cry out to a nanny for comfort, that logic was kept hidden away behind his wife's own needs.

"Caleb...I'm here. I'll help you. I'll always help you." Kevin was crying, his voice shaky. "But you can't go up there, son. She is very hurt. We have to get out of the jet, okay?"

"Get Carmen, Dad. Help her!"

Kevin was at a crossroads. Does he lie to his son and continue making light of the carnage a mere twelve feet from them? Or does he present the ugly truth and let him see for himself that things are as bad as they appear. This wasn't rated PG. This wasn't even R. This was far beyond any rating. These images scar forever. They won't make his son fear the water. They'll make him fear life itself.

"Listen to me, Caleb. You need to do everything I say. I'm going to unbuckle you, and we're going to open that door over there and you're going to go out and stand—"

Kevin looked outside to see if they'd landed on the shore. All he saw was a green curtain of foliage, like being stuck in a carwash made of trees. "Just stand outside. I'm going to get Mom and Melanie, Mrs. Robertson, and...I'm gonna help everyone, then we'll meet you out there. Don't go anywhere, just stand there and don't move."

Caleb was staring at Carmen and the shirt spread across her face, at Ross facedown. He looked at Melanie, Jennifer who was slumped with her head nearly in her lap, and his mom who was stirring awake.

"Why do we need to get out of the plane? Is it going to blow up?"

Kevin hadn't considered why, but when asked, he realized it had everything to do with protecting his son from those scars, from having to look at loved ones in unnatural positions, bleeding. Dead.

"No. I don't think it's going to blow up. Just do what I say, son."

Caleb nodded.

Kevin struggled with the seatbelt a moment before it broke free, then he went to the door and studied the latch, read the instructions written in red. After understanding how it worked, he unlatched the door, but the branches wouldn't allow for it to drop as it should. He and Caleb shoved and kicked, the door giving more with each attempt, until it finally dropped open, forming a small staircase to the jungle floor.

The jungle was dense, and it dawned on Kevin this was not some Miami park you could just stroll through without fear of being mauled, infected, or stung by exotic animals or insects. This was the Caribbean, and from the view before they crashed, it appeared uninhabited.

Kevin quickly changed his mind that exiting the jet was their best first move, so went to shut the door but couldn't figure out how. "Face the back of the Jet, Caleb."

He did, watching his mother rub at her head and neck.

"I'm going to help Mr. Robertson. Just keep an eye on your mom."

Kevin left his son there and went to Ross, turning him slightly. His nose was broken, his face colored

red. Kevin grabbed his friend by the feet and pulled him out of the doorway and into the short aisle between the seats, then headed back to the cockpit.

The controls may as well have been the motherboard of a spaceship. The choice of knobs, switches, and dials was intimidating. He studied words where there were any, trying to make sense of them, then grabbed the radio receiver and began flipping switches and pushing buttons, while speaking into the receiver. There was no static, no blips, or beeps. It was broken.

Before he left the cockpit, just to make sure, he checked the pilot's pulse, then Carmen's. The cooling skin of their wrists told him what he already knew. He looked back, made sure Caleb wasn't watching, then grabbed Carmen's legs and moved them, flipping her over and getting her out of the way of the cockpit door, then shut it.

"Kevin?" Vicki's voice was ragged, full of confusion. "Oh, thank God, Caleb."

Caleb ran to his mother and hugged her.

She groaned from the weight of him and put a hand to her ribs. "Is everyone okay?" Vicki asked, then saw Ross on the floor. She looked at Melanie, then Jennifer. "They're...dead?"

Kevin went to Jennifer, felt her pulse. "No, they're fine. Alive anyway."

"I think my ribs are broken." She looked around again, searching. "Where's Carmen?"

Kevin just shook his head, saying the words without speaking.

Jennifer sat up quickly and gasped, as though emerging from deep under water. Her eyes went wide when she saw her husband. Frantically, she unbuckled her belt and ran to him. "Ross!"

Kevin joined her, speaking calmly. "I think he's okay, Jen. Probably looks worse than it is."

She collapsed on top of her husband, her face in the nape of his neck. "Honey, wake up." She sat up, grabbed his arms, and shook him violently, pleading with him.

Kevin placed a gentle hand on Jennifer after seeing Melanie awake, staring at her bloodied father while her mother lost control. "I'll take care of him, Jen. How about you go see how Melanie's doing."

A look of shock struck her as she seemed to realize she hadn't checked her daughter. "Oh, Melanie." She swung her head around, saw her daughter sitting there in a daze, and ran to her.

"What in God's name are we going to do, Kevin?" Vicki asked. "Do we even know where we are?"

Kevin propped Ross up using a pillow he'd found in one of the seats. If Ross was still bleeding, he didn't want him aspirating any blood. "Don't have the first clue. But from the looks of it, I don't think we're anywhere near civilization."

"Will they come looking for us? Like...track the plane somehow?"

"I can't answer that, Vicki. I don't know how any of it works. We could be rescued in half an hour. Or we could be here the rest of our lives. I just don't know."

"Ross needs a doctor." Jennifer said. "He needs a hosp—" She stopped. "Where's Carmen?"

Kevin looked at his son. It was getting more difficult to hide the truth.

"Kevin. Where is Carmen?"

"She's in the cockpit," His eyes still on Caleb, debating on what to say next.

"Is she using the radio? Does it work? Does she know how—"

"She's dead," Vicki's voice was a high-pitched whine, a mouse with its foot caught in a trap.

Kevin watched his son's face contort, creating a mask of grief. The scars were forming. He wondered how alone his son must feel in that moment, hearing the clarifying words that the most precious person in his life was gone. The void filler. The mother and the father. The best friend.

Jennifer broke down and squeezed her daughter, who continued to stare ahead, motionless and in her own world where none of this was happening. Blood was not running, people were not crying, shaking, rubbing their wounds.

"I can't breathe," Vicki said. "I'm suffocating. I'm fucking suffocating." She unbuckled the seatbelt and tore at her blouse. Buttons flew. She got up from the seat and went for the door.

Kevin stopped her. "You can't go out there."

"I have to, Kevin. I can't fucking breathe."

"We don't know what's out there. We're safer in here."

She looked at him like he was the one who'd lost his mind. "We don't know what's out there? I'll tell you what's out there, a shitload of trees and water."

"I mean the wildlife. Some of these animals, they're dangerous. Snakes, alligators, wild boars."

"Well, right now I don't give a shit." She pulled away from him, grunting from the pain in her side, and headed through the leafy curtain and down the stairs.

"Mom!" Caleb yelled.

"Caleb. Stay there, buddy."

"I'll talk to her." Jennifer wiped tears from her face.

"It's not safe, Jen."

"She needs me. I can calm her down. Just keep an eye on my husband, please." The word husband came out fragile and shaky. Kevin could tell she was doing everything she could to hold it together.

"Don't wander off. Stay by the jet."

Jennifer assured her newly-mute daughter she would be right back, then kissed and hugged the girl before heading out.

Kevin spotted Melanie's plush gorilla near the cockpit and grabbed it. He set it in her lap and put her limp arms around it.

"We're going to be okay," he said. "Someone will find us. They have people whose job it is to help in situations like this."

"You told Mom we might be here forever," Caleb said.

Kevin contemplated his next words and wondered whether or not his son would be able to tell it was all bullshit. "Yes, I did say that, and I'm sorry. I didn't mean it. I was just frustrated. We're leaving this island. And when we do, you know that bike you wanted, the one Jack Meyer has? I'm getting you one just like it. Mag wheels, double gooseneck, everything." The words felt like trying to slap a Band-Aid on an amputated leg.

"Is Carmen really dead? Or did Mom drink too much?"

The question caught Kevin by surprise. Not because it was so matter of fact, and not because it put him in the position to spill more truth he didn't want to. It was because he'd never realized just how aware Caleb was of all that was wrong in their lives.

Or did Mom drink too much?

What else did Caleb know? Did he know just how bad their marriage was, and why? Did he know about Carmen's infatuation? Did he pick up on it? Did she tell him by way of clues he was never meant to understand?

"I'm so sorry, Caleb. She really is gone." Kevin felt like there should be more to give, some verbal offering that would help stop the pain. But there was nothing. His words were a stone dropped down an empty well.

A better father could think of the right words.

Maybe. But Kevin knew that while everyone eventually succumbs to death, and often experiences loss before that day comes, they're not built for it. It just happens. They're thrown in the deep-end and do what they can to keep swimming, as the water turns to mud and the ease of movement slows to a crawl as they make their way to the edge, where they hope beyond all that there's someone there with the right words to offer a helping hand. Kevin wanted so desperately to be that hand for his boy.

As he looked into his son's innocent eyes, listening to the muffled whimper of his wife just outside, Ross moaned behind him.

Kevin scrambled to his friend's side. "Hey, buddy."

Ross opened his eyes, fluttered his lids, trying to focus on the figure beside him. The taste of copper filled his mouth, and his head pulsed. It felt like someone was stepping on his face, holding him down with a heavy boot. He touched his nose and winced. It was impossible to breathe through.

53

"Jen's okay, so is Melanie," a voice said. "How do you feel?"

"Where's Jen?"

"She's outside with Vicki."

"How's Luis?"

"Who?"

"The pilot."

"He didn't make it...neither did Carmen."

Ross's eyes flew open. "They're dead?" He sat up, grunting, and grabbed his head.

"Woah. Slow down, man. We're in no hurry."

"I just can't believe this. I mean...a stroke? What are the chances?" He shook his head, fighting the reality of the situation, then looked up at Melanie and could tell right away she was traumatized.

Kevin helped his friend up and walked him to the seat next to Melanie. Ross tucked his daughter's hair behind her ear and pressed his lips against her face, whispering to her. "Hey, honey. Daddy's okay. So is Mommy." He finished the kiss and looked at her slack arms resting around the plush ape. "Looks like

Foozoo's okay too, especially with you taking care of him." He tried to smile.

The girl said nothing.

Ross spoke about the waste of worry and how they'll be rescued soon because people were already out looking for them. He believed none of what he preached.

"I don't suppose you know where we're at," Kevin said.

"Wish I did. I know it's nowhere near Barbados. I'm not even sure we're as far as Guadeloupe." Ross touched his nose again, feeling the bruised fragility of it, picking at the crusting blood carefully. "Then again, flight paths aren't set in a straight line. We could be as far south as Grenada. You take a peek outside yet?"

"Peek is about all I did. I'm a little concerned about the wildlife here."

"I think as long as we keep an eye out for snakes, maybe some of the monkeys...hell...I'm not sure what's out there."

"I checked the radio. As far as I can tell, it's broken."

Ross was half listening. He could hear the timbre of his wife's voice outside. In that moment, it was the most beautiful sound he'd ever heard—a bird's sweet song carried by a cool breeze on a summer day. The sound brought him to his feet and out the door.

They could see the blue of the sea about one hundred yards from where they stood, but a look around in every other direction offered nothing but dense jungle.

Vicki seemed to have calmed down, and her breathing relaxed, though she winced when taking a deep breath. Kevin checked her ribs. They were bruised at the very least. If they were broken, he couldn't feel where. That was a good sign.

He checked the damage of the jet and searched the ground around it. "Not to alarm anyone, but I think it'd be a good idea if we each had something to use as a weapon. If you see any loose hardware in the wreckage, grab it."

"Being armed against a snake is the least of my worries," Vicki said.

"Kevin's right," Ross said. "It's best to be safe. We don't know what's out here."

Out of the corner of his eye, Kevin saw movement in the cockpit window. A shadow, a reflection.

He ran to the door, pushed through the branches, and entered. Vicki called out behind him. He immediately noticed that Caleb wasn't in his seat. He was standing in the doorway of the cockpit. Staring. Making the deepest of scars.

"Caleb!" He grabbed his son's arms, pulled him away from the door, and shut it, then hugged him.

He tried to think of something he could do to erase the images from his son's mind, but mentioning anything but the here and now seemed trivial, perhaps even damaging. He wanted to bring up the time they went fishing (the one and only time) and Caleb had caught the biggest fish. He'd felt so proud, holding it up while his dad took a picture. Or when he won first place at the spelling bee, and afterward they went out for ice cream, where Caleb had helped a woman find her tiny dog that'd wandered off. He saw the nametag on the dog's collar with a phone number attached, then asked for a quarter to use the payphone.

But Kevin knew those recollections meant nothing to him now, and perhaps even bringing them up in this moment would taint them—the sight of a maimed loved one attaching itself like a leech to the otherwise pleasant memories.

They turned toward the door and Vicki was there, hands to her mouth, tears in her eyes. "Oh, honey." She took Caleb's hand in hers and led him outside.

Kevin went to Melanie and knelt down. "How about you come outside with us, honey." She stood, still emotionless, and made movement toward the door with Foozoo in her hand, as though led by something out of her control—a marionette on strings with a shuffling stride.

When they were outside, Ross led his daughter away from the group so the adults could talk in private. He set her on top of a large rock, then went to the others a mere ten feet away, far enough to speak quietly without striking even more fear into her.

While Caleb stood off to the side, closer to the jet, the others stood together, contemplating their options and whether or not they really had any.

"What about the radio?" Vicki asked.

"Doesn't work," Kevin said. "None of the electronics work. No lights, nothing."

Vickie put her hand over her brow as though it helped see further. "I find it hard to believe there's no village or town out here somewhere."

"I don't know about that," Ross said. "There's a lot of islands in the Caribbean, not all of them inhabited."

Jennifer was looking at her daughter. "I'm worried about Melanie."

They all looked at the girl sitting on the rock, expressionless, empty.

Ross grabbed his wife's hand "It's just shock, honey. She's gonna be fine. You know how she is. Can't even watch Scooby Doo without getting spooked."

"This isn't a cartoon, Ross. This is real trauma."

"I know…I'm sorry." He squeezed her hand tight, and they embraced.

Kevin and Vicki looked at each other. Kevin was sure the synchronized glance was because the Robertson's had something they wish they did. Understanding, acceptance, patience. Unconditional love.

"A boy!" Caleb yelled. He was pointing at Melanie.

The four of them swung their heads toward Melanie and saw a teenaged boy about the age of eighteen, shirtless with unkempt, dirty-blonde hair standing directly behind her on the other side of the rock.

"Oh, thank God," Vicki said.

Kevin gave a sigh of relief.

"Our plane just crashed, and we need help," Ross said.

"Thank you, God," the boy said, then raised a hammer in the air and brought it down on the back of Melanie's head with a loud crack. She collapsed with rolling eyes, and the boy grabbed her by the hair, threw a rope around her neck, then kicked at something behind the rock, which squealed—all within seconds, as though he'd done it a hundred times before.

A chorus of terrifying screams filled the air, as a large wild boar fashioned with a harness raced into the jungle, dragging Melanie's lifeless body behind it, while the boy chased after.

Ross and Kevin sprang forward, when another boy, looking no more than eight years old, jumped in front of them with a makeshift spear in hand. He wore long dreadlocks tied behind his head and tight denim shorts which looked at least one size too small. His spear was decorated with tassels made from what Kevin assumed was hair.

He stabbed at Kevin and missed. Kevin lunged, and the boy dodged the effort, sending Kevin to the ground, where he felt a sharp pain as the boy poked a hole in his shoulder.

Another boy, more like a young man, possibly as old as twenty, wearing a loin cloth made from flimsy hide, went after Ross with a spear in one hand and a hammer in the other. He stuck Ross in the side, tearing his shirt and puncturing the skin. As quick as the spear went in, he pulled it out and took another jab. Ross tripped trying to avoid the attack and fell on his back, clacking his teeth around his tongue. Once again, his mouth filled with the taste of blood.

Vicki dropped to her knees and pulled at her face with a maddening shriek.

The squeals from the pig grew distant as Melanie was taken further and further away from her parents.

Jennifer ran in the direction of the boar's cry, and the young man stabbed her in the arm with a quick strike, knocking her to the ground. With a howl of laughter, both boys joined the first and disappeared into the jungle, leaving no trail behind.

"Melanie!" Jennifer screamed. "Ross...get her! Get my baby!"

Ross stood, holding his side, and ran for the jungle, while Kevin grabbed Caleb and held him close, terrified that another would take his boy.

Ross ran for about ten yards before Kevin watched him disappear into the earth, letting out a scream.

"Take Caleb and get in the jet," Kevin said to Vicki.

The two ran to the jet, and Kevin followed. Once they were inside, he pushed the door up and latched it securely.

Ross shouted again, and Kevin followed the sound until he came upon an eight-foot hole filled with bamboo that had been sharpened to a point and stuck in the ground at the bottom—a trap that Ross somehow managed to avoid except for the fall.

"Get me outta here." Using one of the bamboo spikes to boost himself up, Ross clawed at the dirt around the top of the hole.

With Kevin's shoulder burning with pain, he grabbed his friend's hands and pulled him up and out of the hole.

Jennifer caught up to them. "We can't stop. We have to find her!"

She searched the jungle with frantically darting eyes. "Melanie!" Then sprinted forward, running as fast as she could.

Ross stood, ignoring his bleeding wounds. "Jen! Don't!"

But Jen sank into the earth somewhere ahead of him. There was no scream, only the unmistakable sound of impalement.

Chapter 8

Melanie's head bounced off the jungle floor as the boar ran. All three boys caught up to it, one in front, leading the way.

After a few minutes, they reached a clearing filled with tall grass, and the boar stopped. Melanie's face was covered in blood, the skin under her chin raw, her neck clearly broken.

A snake slithered nearby, and the young man stuck it through the head with his spear. The snake writhed and whipped as dirty hands grabbed its neck, found purchase under broken skin, and peeled it back, stripping it free. He stuck the skin over the spear like a sheath, then tossed the carcass into the grass.

The three boys crouched in the grass and watched the jungle behind them.

"This is a different kind of game," the youngest boy with the dreadlocks said.

"So many of them," said the one who'd hit Melanie.

The young man squinted. "Maybe too many."

"We'll go back and take them one at a time. Bring Cain and Abel with us, maybe Adam too." the youngest said.

The young man gave an irritated look. "You know Adam doesn't hunt."

"Maybe he will because there are so many."

"We will do it. We'll make them proud. New clothing, plenty of food."

"Most of it will have to be salted. It's too much. It will rot."

The young man smiled. "You're learning, Abraham. Mother will be proud."

Abraham smiled, then smacked the boar on its ass. The beast took off, violently yanking Melanie with it.

Chapter 9

Ross was on his knees at the edge of the hole where his wife stood upright, skewered by bamboo. One of the spikes ran through her chin and out her neck, while another went through her stomach and out her back.

This hole was deeper than the one Ross had fallen in, each of them having been covered by a collection of leaves, grass, and twigs, rendering them invisible.

"What is happening!?" Ross screamed.

Kevin was there, his hands on Ross's shoulders, squeezing. "We have to get back to the jet." He took note of the sky growing darker. "Ross...we have to go."

"Wake me up, Kev. Please wake me up."

Kevin put his arms under his friend's and lifted, helping him up. Hesitantly, Ross allowed it and began to walk blindly toward the jet, while Kevin was mindful of where they stepped.

Ross's face was a lifeless mask that hung slack. "What happened, Kev? What happened to my girls?"

Once again, Kevin had no words. He couldn't tell him that things would be okay, that somehow his daughter was still alive, because things would never be okay, and they'd all seen the way the girl's neck snapped when pulled from the rock.

"I don't even know what to say, Ross. I'm sorry…but right now we need to focus on protecting ourselves and getting off this island."

"I love those girls so much." Ross let crimson drool fall from his mouth, while his face morphed into a frown that looked as though it'd been carved into him. "They're my whole world."

"They're good girls." Kevin wasn't comfortable speaking of them in the past tense. Ross wasn't doing it. And probably wouldn't for some time. Past tense was filled with too much admittance, too much reality. Denial felt like a healthy mode in that moment, and he'd dwell in it for as long as Ross needed him to.

They reached the jet, and Ross wandered over to the rock. "I just *had* to put her here…away from safety…away from my protection."

"You set her there *for* her protection. You were looking out for her, keeping her ears covered. It would have been cruel to have her listening to us...the adults who are supposed to have everything figured out. She was in no condition to hear the fear in our voices."

"But you kept Caleb near."

"Maybe I shouldn't have. But after Carmen, I just thought...I don't know, Ross. I mean...how do you protect your child from tragedy like this, you know? This isn't Grandma on her death bed. This is premature. It's visceral and senseless."

Ross just stared at the dying sun as it painted the sky pink, and Kevin thought the man might be perfectly content having his eyes burn out right then and there.

"We need to get to the luggage. Vicki packed a few snacks for Caleb. It ain't much, but we should eat. Plus, we need to make a rope. I don't know how to get that door shut from the inside. I figure we could tie—"

"Did you sleep with Carmen?" Ross said.

It was the last thing Kevin expected to hear. "I did. Once. It was a huge mistake."

"Mistakes happen." Ross kept his eyes on the sun.

"But they're never worth it."

"No, I suppose they're not."

Kevin made sure he was the one to access the luggage, keeping Melanie and Jennifer's inside and away from Ross. Kevin grabbed the snacks (consisting of a box of cookies and two small bags of potato chips) and threw on a T-shirt, then they made a rope by tying a few of his other shirts and a sheet together. Vicki had insisted on bringing her own sheets on the trip, stating she had a hard time sleeping on anything but satin.

After creating the rope, they tied it to the latch and pulled the door shut.

Vicki was in hysterics. She paced, asking more than once if Ross had brought any alcohol. Kevin began to wish they had, anything to calm her down.

The two men tended to their wounds the best they could. They weren't life-threatening but could eventually face infection. Ross folded a clean sock and placed it directly over the small hole in his side, then tied a long piece of cloth around his waist he made from one of his shirts.

Kevin's shoulder was sore, affecting his range of motion. He wiped it down, but there wasn't much else he could do.

"We never should have taken this stupid plane. We should have flown commercial. But you had to act like Daddy Warbucks, like some kind of rich asshole."

"That's not fair, Vicki," Ross said.

"If anyone should be pissed off, it should be you. Look at what's happened to your family."

"That's not Kevin's fault, and you know it." Ross caught her eye, then looked at Caleb, signaling that now was not the time. Not in front of her son.

"I heard what Carmen said." Vicki's eyes narrowed at Kevin.

"What do you mean?" Kevin said.

"Just before we crashed, I heard her."

"What in the f—" He looked at Caleb, then lowered his voice. "What are you talking about, Vicki?"

"She said she loved you, that she's always loved you."

"That makes no sense. She never said that, and I hardly think this is the time to—"

"You were fucking her."

Caleb brought his knees to his chest and covered his ears.

"Vicki…"

"How could you do that to me...to Caleb."

Hearing Vicki play the victim sent a flash of rage through him, no longer being able to control his tongue, even in the presence of his 9-year-old son. "You gotta be kidding me. How could I do that to you? Let's talk about your boss, Larry. Let's talk about all those late nights at work."

Vicki's face grew pale, and her entire demeanor changed. She was no longer on the attack. She was a tiny mouse, stomped under foot after having bitten the lion.

"How about our old neighbor, Jim Tenny, and his mother who just happened to need a nurse's aid every Thursday around 10:00."

Vicki said nothing, could say nothing.

"Caleb is the only reason I still walk through that front door and sleep in that bed, so don't you fucking dare talk to me about tearing this family apart when you've been trying to do that for the last eight years. Hell, the only thing you haven't tried yet is fucking Ross."

Between the sun going down and the coverage of trees, the inside of the jet had grown dark. But not dark enough to miss Ross and Vicki trading guilty glances.

Kevin's gut filled with lava. "You can't be serious." He looked at Ross, who threw his eyes to the floor in shame and began to cry.

Vicki folded her arms and looked out the window, covered by a blast of dark green.

Kevin wanted to storm out, but he couldn't. He was needed. His son was broken, quietly sobbing. And as mad as he was at Ross for the unspeakable betrayal, the man had just lost everything. Sure, their book would never be written, and their friendship would end. But until they got off the island, he would be there for them all. Everything else, no matter how sinister, felt trivial now.

"I'm sorry, Kevin," Vicki reached a hand out and Kevin stood up, backed away.

"I don't wanna hear it. I don't wanna talk about it. We've got other shit to worry about."

Ross stared at the ground and shook his head, remained quiet.

"Okay…" Kevin said, trying to collect himself with a deep breath. "Back to these fuckers in the jungle. Let's think about who we're dealing with here."

"Natives?" Vicki offered. "Some undiscovered tribe?"

Kevin was instantly irritated with her reply, like she hadn't been paying attention out there. "They spoke English, Vicki. They had a fuckin' hammer and clothes."

She shut down.

"They're savages is what they are," Ross said. "I can't explain the English or anything else, but they're not living in an apartment somewhere half a mile away, that's for damn sure. They live right here...in the jungle."

Kevin took a moment to think, to come up with answers.

"Maybe…" Caleb's timid voice cut the silence. "Maybe they crashed here too once. And this is how they survive."

"No." Kevin was quick to shut the idea down. Entertaining it felt like just another way of admitting they were doomed, that this was the place they would die, even though the boy's theory was the only logical thing any of them had come up with. "That's not what happened. It's something else. If they were survivors from some shipwreck or plane crash, they would have been found before it came to this. It's something else."

He and Ross traded glances, knowing the theory could be possible.

"I think we should follow the shore in the morning. There's a chance these are outcasts, living on the outskirts of a town, like vagrants," Ross said.

A bright orange glow passed along the walls of the jet. Kevin was the first to notice and went to a window.

Near the rock were four figures, two of them holding torches.

Chapter 10

Mother Eve sat on the floor of the hut next to a small torch stuck in the ground that lit the room. She watched her youngest—3-year-old Miriam—stack misshapen wooden blocks atop one another, each with a number on it. The girl stacked them in order from one to three, then held numbers four and five in her hands, deciding which came next.

"Ooone, twooo, threee...then what?" Eve asked.

"This one?" Miriam held up the block that had the number four on it.

Eve clapped and shouted approval, and her daughter set the block on top of the others.

The hut consisted of two large rooms made from thin trees, heavy leaves, palms, reeds, and bamboo held together by sinew and thin, ropey vines. The structure resembled those Eve had seen on a TV show as a child, where a group of people were stranded on an island, making the best of it. Just like she had done for the past twenty years. The first few years were a confusing struggle filled with heartache and loneliness, but eventually the island beat her into submission, and she accepted her new way of life. Before long, memories of normalcy were nothing more than dream-like visions of something that barely ever existed. Perhaps the first twelve years of her life, somewhere else, off the island, were nothing more than creations from her own mind, triggered by a life of solitude. She could no longer tell.

Ten-year-old Hannah entered the hut. She wore a tattered skirt with no shirt. Her curly hair hung down her back in sandy-blonde tendrils bleached by the sun.

"When will they be back?" she asked her mother.

"Tonight. Are you worried?"

"A little."

Eve patted the ground next to her. "What are you worried about?"

The girl sat down. "Noah said God was playing a different kind of game. That maybe there are too many."

"God is blessing us."

"But it's too much. What will we do with it all?"

It was a question Eve had asked herself. Salting the meat was an option, but this much? How many had Abraham said there were? Six? Maybe more? Unless they were small children, God had never given them more than one at a time.

"And what if they hurt us like they did Father?"

"Your father is foolish. He was showing off. And we all learned from it, didn't we?" She was speaking of two years ago, when Adam had hunted a full-grown man by himself. The man was bigger, more agile, resulting in Adam losing an eye and a permanent limp. Afterward, the tribe's respect for him dwindled, especially when Noah, who was only sixteen at the time, finally took the prey down, cracking his spine with a single blow from a hammer while the man slept.

"It's still too many. I don't like it." Hannah stormed out of the hut.

Eve certainly wouldn't admit it to her daughter, but she was right. This was something new for them. Was it a test? Or did others come to wipe them out and take their home?

Adam staggered out of the other room, his left lid sunken where an eye once dwelled. "The boys need to stay away. They will end up dead."

"They're careful, and they're strong. They don't go out alone," Eve bit back.

"They practice foolishness when your back is turned."

It was true, at times they were careless, but they never went alone. Not like Adam.

"There is only one fool here. One half man."

Adam glared at the woman and snarled his lip, then left the hut and walked over to a hole in the sand near the shore and relieved himself. When he was done, he kicked sand into the hole and walked back to the hut.

"The one they brought in needs gutting," Eve said.

The man said nothing but went to the next room and grabbed a knife. It was dull from years of use, but dependable. He went back outside and found the young girl with the broken neck hanging upside down from the usual tree. She'd already been scalped. Most likely Hannah's doing. She often used the hair to make dolls for her and Miriam.

He grabbed the girl by the arm so she wouldn't swing, then plunged the knife in her just above the pubic bone and opened her wide.

Chapter 11

"They're just standing there." Vicki was looking out one of the jet windows.

Kevin recognized three of them as being the same ones from earlier.

"I need you to do me a favor." Ross gripped Kevin's shoulder firmly, looked him in the eyes. "I'm going out there. You'll have to shut the door behind me."

"They'll kill you."

"I need to do this, Kevin. For my girls."

"No way. You don't even have a weapon."

Ross looked at the seats, the aisle. "There's gotta be something in here." He ran to the cockpit and opened it. The smell of feces and urine filled the air, a reek that confused him until he remembered the morbid prank death pulls after it takes you. It was darker in the cockpit than the rest of the jet. "Do we have a light?"

"Doesn't matter, Ross. You're not going out there. Anything you find in here as a weapon won't have the reach those spears do."

"I have a lighter," Vicki said.

Ross ran back, got the lighter from Vicki. When he flicked it at the entrance to the cockpit, the sight of the bluing bodies within shook him still. Luis was bent over as though drunk, his face discolored where the blood had pooled. Then he saw Carmen, her jaw ripped open, her neck grotesquely crooked.

On the floor between the pilot's seat and the console was a gym bag crammed in the tight space. Ross grabbed it, shut the door, and ran back to the others.

Vicki was glued to the window. "They're talking, but I can't tell what they're saying."

Ross unzipped the bag and pulled out a hand towel, two dirty magazines, a candy bar, can of cashews, and a flare gun. "Hot damn!"

"Tell me you're not thinking of wasting that flare on them," Kevin said.

"It's no waste...I know exactly what this is. Researched these when I was writing *In a Midnight Sky*. This isn't just any flare gun, Kev. This is *thee* flare gun, 26.5 mm. None of that weak 12-gauge shit. Luis must have been in the military. No way this is regulation."

"Looks pretty old."

"It's decades old."

"How many flares?"

"Two. If we hit one of them with this, they're done. The rest of 'em see that, they'll probably haul ass outta here."

Something heavy hit the window where Vicki sat watching.

She screamed, then scrambled across the aisle and to another seat. "They threw a rock."

More rocks hit the jet—the metal, the windows.

Caleb ran to his mom, who'd curled up on the seat. "Will that break the windows?"

"Eventually, but it'd take a hell of a lot. They're not glass," Kevin said.

"I'm going out." Ross held the flare gun firmly in one hand, the extra flare in the other. "Shut the door behind me."

"Don't do it, Mr. Robertson!" Caleb yelled.

"Ross...the chances of you making it back aren't good. We're protected in here. They can hit the jet all night and won't get to us."

"You don't get it...I'm not worried about making it back. If I don't kill one of those bastards, I'm gonna lose my mind. Now...shut the door behind me." Ross grabbed the latch and opened the door. Before he was able to take a step down, a rock hit him in the head and the flare gun went off, striking the roof of the jet and ricocheting down toward the bathroom, where it burned bright for the next ten seconds.

Caleb and Vicki both ducked in their seats and covered their heads.

Kevin stripped the gun and extra flare from Ross's hands, loaded the flare. Another rock flew, sailing past Kevin and hitting the window behind him. He raised the gun and aimed at one of the boys who held a torch.

Kevin pulled the trigger, and the flare hit its target, burying itself in the boy's chest. The kid flew back, dropping the torch, and fire exploded where the flare remained buried.

The rocks stopped, and one of the boy's screamed, "Abraham!" Then, just as Ross had predicted, they ran, howling the dead boy's name along the way.

Chapter 12

Terror struck them all. Noah, Cain, and Abel. They ran recklessly through the jungle, barely being mindful of their own traps. This had never happened before, losing one of their own. The closest they'd come was Adam and his prideful hunt.

"I said too many. I said it!" Noah yelled.

"It wasn't too many. It was the weapon," Abel said.

Not another word was spoken as they ran home, where the rest of their tribe waited for their return, anticipating the feast God had blessed them with.

Chapter 13

Kevin shut the door, and watched the body burn from the window. It was the youngest boy. His dreads splayed out and glowing as the fire ran through them like wicks, a smoldering hole in the child's chest.

Ross sat holding his forehead. It'd been split by the rock, adding blood to his already rusted face. "He was mine, dammit!"

"It doesn't matter who did it," Kevin said. "What matters is they're gone."

"It damn well matters to me."

"They would have killed us, Ross. I had to do something."

"I'm a failure. I didn't protect my daughter...my wife. I betrayed my best friend. And when I get a chance at revenge, I fuck that up too."

"Listen, man. You got your revenge. You came up with the plan. It was a good plan. It worked."

Kevin understood the man's grief and knew there was no consoling him. When you're that deep in, you look for more reasons to bury yourself deeper. Only the passing of time can dig you out.

Vicki grabbed the empty gym bag and went through it like a racoon looking for scraps. Or alcohol.

"How about we dig into the food we have." Kevin started arranging the nuts, chips, candy bars, and cookies in a pile. "We'll split this into fourths. Caleb, come get some of this."

"I'm not hungry."

"I'm not either, son. But we need to eat. We'll be walking a lot tomorrow."

"Then I'll eat tomorrow."

"Isn't there fruit on these islands? Like mangos and bananas?" Vicki said.

"Most likely, unless the tribe has cleaned them out."

Ross found himself a seat and reclined, stared at the ceiling.

"Okay, so nobody's gonna eat?" Kevin said.

Silence.

"Alright then. We'll save it for breakfast."

Each of them had chosen a seat away from the others, spread out like men at the urinals in a restroom. It seemed even Caleb didn't want to be near his parents. Kevin wondered if it was because it felt like picking sides. Every secret was out now. He'd slept with Carmen. His wife had slept with everyone. If Caleb felt alone earlier, now he truly was, with the inability to trust anyone.

Kevin laid his head back and tried not to think how he'd just killed a young boy, as the smell of burning hair and flesh wafted in from somewhere.

Chapter 14

Eve was the only one to cry after hearing of Abraham's death.

The other children were worried it would happen to them too, and Adam was disappointed in the older boys for letting it happen. To Eve, it felt like his way of saving face and wondered if he didn't feel some relief knowing the story of him being bested by his prey would no longer be the example of what not to do. She'd sensed a desperation in Adam the past year, thinking he may be capable of anything just to gain respect once again, and if part of that was celebrating the death of their son, so be it.

She was even more confused now by what God had done and why, still torn between believing it may be a test and them purposely being wiped out. Part of her wanted the tribe to be laid to waste. A very small part of her, a conviction she hadn't felt in nearly twenty years.

As she listened to the children speak of tactics and vengeful planning, she felt alone in her own way of thinking, as though somehow they'd all done something very wrong. But why would this feeling come now? Was it the death of her son that brought about this new irrational thinking? Or was it something that'd been tucked away all these years, while she taught—with the writings given by God— every member of the tribe how to build, how to speak and read, how to prepare the prey for cooking or salting, as well as how to hunt every living being let loose.

But what is God doing?

She speculated, contemplated, and listened, as her children sat by the fire and feasted on the arms of the girl God had given them.

Chapter 15

No one slept well except for Caleb, who crashed hard once the rush of adrenaline subsided. The others tossed, turned, and gazed out the windows, waiting for an ambush. But none came. The night was uneventful.

Come morning, Ross was the first up. His face itched from the crusted blood, and he wanted nothing more than to hit the sea and rinse off, maybe even drink the water, judging for himself whether or not it was a good idea. He'd always learned it was not. But there wasn't a single beverage on the jet.

He sat quietly in the seat, listening to a multitude of birds he couldn't identify, caressing the lacerated knot on his forehead. He looked out the window and, through the trees, saw the sky lighting up—an otherwise beautiful sight if only he could have shared it with his family.

It was his first sunrise without them.

Kevin stirred awake and joined him. "We should get an early start."

Ross didn't respond. He was lost in what should have been, wondering if maybe he deserved to lose them. They loved him unconditionally, yet he slept with Vicki. Not once, but a half dozen times. He wanted Jennifer to come back if only to scream with rage at him for what he'd done, to beat his broken nose to a pulp. It felt like the only way he'd ever be normal was if she were allowed her own revenge.

Vicki woke, checked on her son, and kissed his head gently. She sat next to Ross and Kevin. "I'll take that food now."

"I was thinking…trying to find some fruit might be a better idea," Kevin said. "Most of what we have is loaded with salt, and those cookies won't go down too well without something to drink."

"I'll take a bite of the candy bar then."

"Go ahead. And give the rest to Ross and Caleb."

Ross raised his hand and shook his head, signifying he didn't want any.

"Let's wake Caleb and head out. We'll bring the flare gun. If we run into the savages again, they don't need to know it's not loaded. And let's find some sticks. Long ones."

After seeing Caleb stare at the dead boy with the hole in his chest and blackened head, Kevin covered the body with giant leaves from the plants that grew nearby, then steered clear of the area.

They searched the ground for sticks, but most were too brittle and short, so they broke live ones from the trees. Kevin was hoping for larger, thicker sticks to swing like baseball bats rather than jab forward like spears, but without the means to cut the branches, they had to settle for thin, making sure they were at least four feet long. They sharpened the ends on the rock where Melanie had lost her life. Ross wept while sharpening his.

Before they set out, Kevin offered the flare gun to Ross, but he declined with a wave of his hand. The man hadn't said a word since they'd left the jet. He walked to the edge of the roughly hewn trail the boar—and then he and Jennifer—had made and looked in the direction where his wife stood upright in a deep hole, impaled by spikes.

"Ross?" Kevin said.

Ross stood silent, breathing hard. Staring.

"Let's see if we can't find some food, okay?" Ross's resistance made Kevin nervous. He could tell his friend wanted to see his wife one last time—like the viewing at a funeral, or at least visit the hole like one might visit a grave, paying his respects. But the risk of hitting yet another trap made the considerate gesture a dangerous one.

Ross broke from his daze and sprinted toward the hole, running past the one he'd fallen in the day before.

"Ross!"

"Ross stop," Vicki cried out.

When he reached the trap where Jennifer died, he jumped, as though doing a cannonball into the pit.

A grunt. Then silence.

Kevin stared in shock at the empty space his old friend had been only a second ago.

Vicki gasped, throwing her hand over her mouth. Caleb dropped to his knees, quivering, squeak-like cries escaping him.

Kevin turned to his family, eyes wide, face full of terror. "I have to make sure he's okay,"

"No...don't go, Kev," Vicki said.

"I know where the traps are. Just stay here."

Wasting no more time, Kevin ran for the hole. Looked in. Ross's head was thrown back, facing the sky with dead eyes. One of the spikes had gone through his armpit, while another had shot through his rectum. The married couple stood together like two broken scarecrows in a sunken field.

"Dammit, Ross." But Kevin understood. In a single day, Ross had lost everything. And the guilt he felt was tremendous. Even if most of it was unwarranted, he'd found a way to dig himself deeper.

The sound of a stick breaking, the crunch of leaves under foot.

Kevin looked up and saw a man with dark skin, a sunken eye, and long dreadlocks peering at him from behind a group of palms. This was no boy.

Run!" Kevin yelled.

Caleb stood up and ran as fast as he could, away from the jet and toward the shore, Vicki followed, spear in hand. Before long, Kevin caught up.

"Keep going! Follow the shore!"

With her free hand, Vicki held her ribs as she ran, while Kevin winced each time his left arm moved, the hole in his shoulder opening. None of them dared look back.

Chapter 16

Adam watched the family run from him. It felt good to be feared. He'd thought of charging the man as he stood there, but he'd seen the other willingly submit to the trap for some reason and wanted to get to him instead.

Or was fear the real reason he didn't charge?

No. The traps need to be emptied, otherwise it was a waste of food. Besides, the prey his boys had brought home was frail and thin, hardly a contribution. The man in the hole was more than adequate.

He limped toward the hole, pulling the boar alongside with a lengthy rope. But when he reached the hole, he saw it had trapped two people, both adults. This would surely gain him respect. He would tell the others he'd killed them, fighting bravely as they wielded the weapon that killed Abraham.

Using the pig's rope, he made a slipknot and dropped it into the trap and around the man's neck, then wrapped the other end around the tree and pulled. Adam's muscles strained against the man's hefty weight. He pulled steadily, carefully, making sure not to yank the rope, as it could tear the head from the body.

Once the man's head poked up from the hole with bulging eyes, Adam wrapped the other end of the rope around a tree limb, then grabbed the man by the arm and waistband, and pulled him out.

After regaining his strength, he repeated the same for the woman, who was much lighter. By the time he was done, his muscles trembled, so he fastened the rope back onto the pig's crude harness and rested against a tree, dozing off for some time.

When he startled awake, the boar was chewing on the man's face, having already plucked the nose and lips. Adam scolded the boar and whacked it with a stick.

He studied the jet from afar. He knew of them, had seen them fly over, remembered them from his old life. But never had he been this close. It was monstrous, intimidating. And he couldn't be sure there weren't more people inside, hiding. But he didn't want to know. He already had two of them— trophies to bring back home.

He wrapped the end of the rope around the man's ankles, then grabbed the woman's wrist, dragging her, and set off toward home, where newly-found respect awaited.

Chapter 17

With sticks in hand, they ran for what must have been two miles, until Vicki threw up and dropped to the sand.

Kevin finally looked behind them. No sign of the man or any other part of the tribe. "We need to keep going." He helped Vicki up.

Their pace slowed but stayed brisk, keeping an eye on the jungle should the tribe cut them off.

Kevin began to question if leaving the safety of the jet was the right thing to do, but the idea of starving to death inside, while potentially being close to help, haunted him. They had to try something.

Another thought mortified him, that he was leading his family into certain death. Away from their safe haven and straight into the belly of the beast. He had no idea where the tribe called home. He could only go by what direction they'd ran the day before—the opposite way Kevin and his family went.

Up ahead, the shore turned inward. They'd be able to see a farther distance once they rounded the bend.

He pointed this out to Vicki, hoping she would be fueled by the optimism that around that foliage lay freedom and safety. It worked. She picked up her pace, charging into a full sprint, leaving Caleb behind her. Kevin hung back alongside his son, silently promising his boy he'd be the best dad anyone's ever had, should they make it out alive.

Vicki rounded the corner and screamed. It wasn't a fearful scream but one of relief. Kevin actually smiled, trusting the scream held promise, that he would get that opportunity to become the dream dad. The one who spent every available moment teaching his boy, sharing his wisdom, his undivided attention and unconditional love.

Vicki disappeared around the corner. "Help!" she screamed. The tone still held promise, like someone was there who could save them and that everything would be okay.

But Kevin recalled the last time they thought that, when Melanie Robertson took a hammer to the head.

Chapter 18

Kevin and Caleb rounded the bend and laid their eyes on a large building that resembled a cube-shaped warehouse. It was completely square, with the bottom half devoid of windows and made from cinderblock. Above that, twenty feet off the ground, the rest of the structure looked more like a house, complete with siding and two windows on each side that sat nearly forty feet apart. A man stood outside the building with a notebook in his hand and the other hand over his brow, looking at Vicki.

"Help!" she screamed again. The man set the notebook down and ran to her. He had a scraggly gray beard and goldfish eyes that sat behind thick glasses. His hair was missing on top, but the rest of his head was covered in wisps of gray brought to a tight ponytail behind his head.

Sporting a white lab coat—that'd seen better days—the man resembled a doctor, and the look on his face was one of shock as he looked at the three of them.

"Simon! Get out here" the man yelled, and within seconds another man came out of the building, saw Vicki, and drew a gun from his side, pointing it at her.

She froze, arms in the air.

"Woah…hey!" Kevin yelled. While the savages who'd killed Melanie were clearly quasi-primitive as opposed to the men before them, he couldn't tell if there was correlation between the two. Why else would a screaming woman in obvious distress be threatened with a gun? Was it because they too had dealings with the tribe and trusted no one? "What the hell is wrong with you people?"

Kevin caught up to his wife. With only twenty feet between himself and the two men, he pushed Caleb behind him, protecting him.

"Lower your gun, Simon." The man looked at Kevin and his family—dirtied and disheveled. "You seem to be having some trouble." He had an accent but not thick enough for Kevin to place it. Perhaps Russian.

"Our plane crashed, and we need…" Vicki trailed off, and Kevin wondered if she was on the verge of saying they needed to get to a hospital because people were hurt. But all the seriously hurt people were dead. Stroked out, ripped apart and broken, impaled, and dragged away.

Kevin took over. "There are people in the jungle...Americans, I think, who killed our friends, and we—"

"Your plane crashed? Did you *mean* to land here?"

"No. We were headed to Barbados, and our pilot had a stroke midflight."

"What of the other pilot?"

"There was no other pilot. We took a private charter."

"I see. So, are you the only survivors?"

It seemed to Kevin these questions could have waited, and he quickly grew irritated. "Yes."

"We haven't had anything to eat or drink," Caleb said.

The man studied Caleb. Smiled. "Well, I think we can take care of that for you." He turned to Simon. "Would you be so kind."

Simon holstered his gun and went inside.

Kevin felt uneasy about the man's demeanor. Calm. Maybe too calm. Either he was not to be trusted, or he didn't share their concern because he knew they were safe.

Vicki looked nervously behind her. "I don't want to stand out here. Can we come inside? These people...they're dangerous. They set traps, and hit poor Melanie on the head with...and a pig…" She broke down and couldn't continue.

"By all means, please come in." He waved them toward the door. "I'm Dr. Barnard."

Kevin didn't bother introducing himself or his family. Considering the circumstances, he was in no mood for formalities.

As they entered the building, Kevin could hear a quiet rumble from somewhere in the distance he assumed was a generator, since there were lights on within the windowless structure.

The space was vast, with three doors along the back wall. Most of the space was empty, with desks in the middle, topped with what looked like computer monitors, and a file cabinet nearby. A deep freezer sat along the far wall with a refrigerator next to that. The side walls were lined with bookshelves and diagrams drawn on posterboard, and bulletin boards with index cards pinned to them, as well as a large map Kevin assumed was the island. It was clear from the little bit he saw that work was being done here, and these men spent a lot of time doing it.

"Can we get some water, please," Vicki said.

"Yes, of course. I believe Simon is taking care of that."

"Do you have anything stronger?"

"Vicki...really?"

"I'm a wreck, Kevin. Hell, we could all use it."

"As a matter of fact, I do have something stronger," Dr. Barnard said. "But perhaps we should get something in your stomach first."

Simon walked out with a half-filled milk jug of water, handed it to Vicki. She grabbed it, guzzled from it, then gave it to Caleb.

Nodding toward the map, Kevin said, "It looks like you're familiar with the island, so can you tell us anything about the people here? I'm having a tough time wrapping my head around any of this. The island looks deserted, yet there's an English-speaking group of savages out there...young ones. And then this place." He spread his arms out. "Is this some sort of research center?"

"Very observant, Mr..."

"Kevin."

"Research is in fact the proper term. We're here studying wildlife, which may sound exciting, but when you've put as many hours in as Simon and myself, it can get a little tedious. Hence the reason for our library over there. Those aren't just nonfiction books you see on the shelves. If the only entertainment came from watching monkeys mate, well we'd have used Simon's gun on ourselves a long time ago." The doctor chuckled.

"And the savages?"

"Not exactly welcoming, are they?"

"This isn't a fucking joke, Doctor. Three people I love were killed, and that doesn't include the two from the crash. With your smug smile and your shit bedside manner, I get the impression you don't understand the seriousness of this...or you just don't care."

The doctor looked like he was trying to bite his tongue. "My apologies. That's not how I intended to come across. Other than Simon, I don't exactly find myself in social situations, so I guess my skills in that area have atrophied."

Caleb handed the water to his father. Kevin downed some, resisting the urge to finish it off.

"So, what's your transport off the island?" Kevin asked.

"We don't have any."

"You can't possibly be stranded here. There must be others that come and relieve your shift, maybe every week, every month."

Dr. Barnard took a handkerchief from the pocket of his lab coat and rubbed his brow, then drew a heavy sigh. "You really do ask a lot of questions, Mr...Kevin. And that's very unfortunate."

Simon drew his gun and pointed it at Kevin.

"Congratulations. You and your family have just become part of the research. What happens now is,

Simon is going to take you back through one of those doors. And if I were you, I'd make no sudden movements. Or he'll put a bullet in the boy's head."

Simon switched targets.

"You're welcome to keep the jug. You'll need it to piss in."

Chapter 19

The twins—Cain and Abel—sat on the ground, each holding a warbler by the wings, spreading them out and making the birds fight one another. Their beaks pecked, and tiny feet kicked, trying to break free. The wings of each bird had broken soon after the fight began and now were nothing more than handles to keep the game going.

When the twins spotted Adam in the distance, limping more than usual and towing God's gifts, they threw the birds and ran to help. Noah ran after and relieved his father of the woman's weight, while the twins freed the man's legs and carried him to the spot dedicated for preparation and dressing—a dirt courtyard surrounded by stones, where tree limbs reached over the circle like clotheslines for hanging flesh meant for salting.

Once the bodies were put in the circle, Hannah wasted no time in retrieving her knife and began carving at the woman's scalp, peeling away her long red hair.

Eve walked out of the hut, little Miriam following close behind. "How many are left?"

"Is that all that matters?" Adam said, clearly agitated. "I've killed two of them. I did what the boys could not."

Eve studied the bodies, saw the missing face, the large hole through the woman's mid-section, the rip in her neck, the man with his crotch bloodied from deep between his legs. These were not killed by Adam. They were trapped.

Noah patted his father's back in congratulations, a job well done.

Eve scowled. "Do not praise the half-man. He killed nothing."

The children looked confused, and Noah quickly pulled his hand from Adam's shoulder, as though taking back his admiration.

Adam screamed with rage and pulled his knife, then brought it down into the back of the boar's neck. The boar squealed and ran, making it only a few feet before its legs gave out and it seized violently in the dirt.

Eve shook her head. "It's the only thing you *can* kill...the defenseless pig who carries your load."

Adam pushed through his sons, making his way to the bodies. He pushed Hannah aside, then ripped at the dead woman's shirt, exposing her breasts. He then plunged the knife into one of the pale mounds with an angry grunt.

Eve assumed this was his way of demonstrating his growing hatred for her, that he longed to do to her what he was doing to the corpse.

He withdrew the knife from the breast, then sawed through the areola, severing the nipple. The children looked on while he embarrassed himself further through his fit of rage and put the nipple in his mouth. He stood and walked to Eve, chewing loudly in her face with exaggerated chomps—his mouth open, filled with stringy webs of saliva. Then he spit the bolus of flesh at her and stormed into the hut.

The children looked at their mother with sympathetic eyes. They all knew their father had let pride rule him, and it had gotten worse.

Eve wiped the bloody spittle from her face. "Cain, Abel...gut the man. Wash the organs and put them in the net, make sure you throw a stone in to keep them under water. Noah, you gut the woman. We'll have what we can from her tonight and salt the rest, along with the man." She bent down so she was eye level with Miriam. "I want you to play with your sister. You can help her make some new dolls."

Before Eve turned to go in the hut and speak with Adam, she said, "And get rid of the man's head. The pig has tainted it."

Cain removed the man's head and tossed it aside, while Abel made a cut along the top of the man's shoulders, down his arms, and to his wrists, then dug his fingers beneath the flesh by his neck and pulled, separating the skin from muscle.

Noah did the same to the woman, though when reaching the breasts he was careful to use the knife to filet the chest without removing muscle or glands.

Miriam laughed as Hannah put the entire scalp of hair over the tiny doll made from a root and dried reeds. It was a joke she did every time to make her sister laugh.

Every child stopped what they were doing and listened when they heard their mother yell.

"Do not forget your place here, half-man," Eve said.

Adam stood with his face to the ground, not out of shame, but disgust. Self-disgust. He was stronger than her, yet he'd allowed himself to be shaped into a timid little man. He hadn't felt the joy of God or his blessings for two years now. He felt betrayed, godless.

"Coming here, claiming you had killed. You are a liar and a fool. Your own children would have figured it out themselves the moment they began gutting them."

Adam snapped.

He grabbed Eve by the hair and brought her head to meet his knee. Her nose crunched from the impact. He then quickly jabbed his thumb into her eye, popping the orb from its socket, covering his hand in blood.

She screamed, and Adam knew the children would come running to her aid. He quickly grabbed his spear and ran from the hut, pushing through the twins on his way out.

Chapter 20

The plywood walls that made up the 8 x 8-foot cell were thick. Kevin had kicked one and wondered if each wall wasn't made from a double-ply of ¾-inch wood. The door was heavy, with a gapped bottom, allowing about three inches from the door to the floor, where trays of food might be passed.

There was only a very small amount of water left, and within an hour, Vicki had to urinate. "Turn your head, Caleb."

He did, while his mother squatted near the door. Thankfully, the puddle of urine carried its pooling momentum under the door and out of the cell.

"Dad? Who are these guys?"

"I'm not sure. Still trying to put the pieces together." But Kevin did have the germ of an idea, though nothing concrete.

He studied the crayon graffiti on the walls and was alarmed by how much of it looked to be from children. There were remnants of passages written that had been sanded away, as though the cell's past inhabitants meant to send informative messages the doctor deemed a threat.

Outside the door, Simon spoke. "Doctor, take a look at this. Adam is angry."

Footsteps.

"Ahh, yes. If I had to guess, he's trying to reclaim his position as alpha...just like an ape. Very interesting. Do we know what led to this?"

"I'll have to check the tape, but look here. Two bodies."

"Those must be from the plane."

"Do you think the tribe could possibly develop new expectations?"

"Perhaps, but more than likely they feel threatened. And it's far more food than they need. I doubt they'll be disappointed when their rations return to normal. But do take note of the date...and keep an eye on Adam. I'm very curious about his sudden outburst. I'd like to think it's not directed toward Eve. If that's the case, we'll have to intervene. She's much more valuable than him, both to us and the tribe."

It was all the clarification Kevin needed.

"Wildlife research my ass," Vicki said.

They're playing God, Kevin thought. And those in the jungle are somehow buying it. Adam and Eve. They've actually named them, this savage tribe they're monitoring.

"What are they going to do with us?" The worry on Caleb's face broke Kevin's heart. He needed to get them out of there at all costs. There had to be some way off the island. These men had a boat or a plane. Or at the very least, means of communication.

"I wish I knew, son." Kevin kept his voice to a near whisper.

Vicki reached her hand out, touched her husband. "You're not saying much, Kevin. Please tell me you have a plan."

Kevin looked around the wooden cell. Other than being allowed to kick at the wall for days until the wood finally gave or nails loosened, there was no way out except through the door. "We wait. Hopefully, they'll feed us. And pissing on the floor is one thing, but I doubt they want us shitting in here. There's only about twenty feet between us and them, and with that gap in the door...yeah, they don't want that. We're far from the first to be in here, so they have protocol, a routine they follow. If that includes bringing us a bucket or taking us to a bathroom, they'll have to open the door."

One thing that troubled Kevin was the doctor and his lackey didn't seem concerned they might be overheard, as though they knew any prying ears would take their secrets to the grave.

Chapter 21

Several hours passed, the three of them taking turns pissing at the door. At one point, Kevin called out, but no one answered, and no more discussions were had between the doctor and his assistant. The only sound was the occasional clacking of a keyboard.

They were being ignored. Neglected.

"Caleb...do you remember the time you found that bird's nest?" Kevin asked.

Caleb's back was to the wall, knees up, arms across them, head down. "Yeah."

"Only a single egg in it...completely abandoned by its mother, and you saved it. You saved that bird's life."

Vicki gave a weak smile. "I remember you asking me how baby birds eat. And the next thing I know, you had dug up worms from the backyard and were chewing them."

Kevin shook his head. "You said the bird would die if you didn't eat the worms first. But as gross as it was, you were right, and later that summer the little guy took flight."

"We're gonna die here," Caleb said, then sniffed with a nose full of runny snot.

Kevin sat up straight. "No we're not. We're gonna do whatever it takes."

Running footsteps outside the door. They grew distant. Then, "Doctor...come quick."

More footsteps back toward the monitors.

"I can't tell what happened, but Adam ran from the hut, and the children ran inside in a panic."

"Dammit! How in the hell are we supposed to keep doing our work if we don't have cameras with microphones? Twenty years ago they couldn't do it, but they sure as hell can now. It's 1980 for crying out loud. The next report we send, demand mic'd cameras. We've gone about as far as we can without them."

"Another thing to consider, sir. I'm not so sure using the boy right now is a good idea."

"Of course it isn't. Things are completely out of control over there. This plane crash has done extensive damage to our operation."

"So...keep the boy for now?"

"If he's to be Abraham's replacement, we'll have to. Keep him fed, and we'll dispose of the parents and put them in the freezer. An overabundance of food from their god will continue to confuse the tribe."

Caleb began sobbing. Vicki crawled to her son and joined him.

They're not just monitoring them, they're creating them. If they plan to drop a young boy into the tribe, they've done it before. Because of their modern clothes and English language, Kevin wondered if they all had completely different lives prior to the tribe. People who were coerced into a new life from a young age, young enough to successfully brainwash over time, like some morbid version of Stockholm syndrome, forcing a blank slate within a cult-like setting.

They planned to plant his son in the tribe and teach him to kill.

Kevin scooted close to his family, put his arms around them in a huddle. "Okay, listen," he whispered. "There's no time to wait for the perfect opportunity. We need to take the first one we can get. These men aren't trained assassins, they're scientists with a gun. The first time that door opens, one of us will have to disarm him."

"How?" Caleb whined.

"Charge him with his back turned, grab his arm if it's at his side. Hell, kick him in the nuts. Just make sure the gun isn't aimed at one of us if you can help it. Once one of us makes the move, the others jump in. And remember...real fights, they're not choreographed. What I mean is...it's not just about throwing punches. Real fights are messy. You bite, scratch, kick. Whatever it takes."

The boy wiped his face. Kevin wanted to tell his son he loved him, wrap his arms around his frail body and squeeze, smell his hair and let the boy cry. But it'd feel like saying goodbye.

Vicki stroked Kevin's arm. "I'm so sorry, honey."

He looked at her. She had been unfaithful so many times. Selfish and bitter. But at one point they had been in love. Inseparable. He couldn't forget that. Would their marriage be the same should they survive the island? No. It would die, fading into nothing but weekly phone calls to make arrangements on where Caleb would stay that weekend, and limp waves from the doorway as Caleb was dropped off at The Dream Dad's house.

He caressed her arm and squeezed. And that was goodbye whether they lived or not.

The footsteps came back. This time they were approaching the door.

Chapter 22

Filled with fury at what Adam had done to their mother, Cain, Abel, and Noah grabbed their weapons, then instructed Miriam and Hannah to stay and look after Eve. Adam was well out of sight, but they could track him, something Noah prided himself in.

They'd never killed one of their own. It was strictly forbidden. But lies and attacking another had never been an issue before. They had a betrayer amongst them, and the rules for dealing with such was a gray area. Neither their mother nor God had presented such a scenario. However, they had learned the teaching of "eye for an eye." Perhaps that's what Adam felt he was doing. It didn't matter. The reason behind Adam's attack was not important. He wasn't rational. Led by pride and selfishness, his actions were unjust and his consciousness fogged. The pride was a poison within the tribe. And it needed to be cleansed.

Chapter 23

Adam wiped the blood from Eve's eye onto his face in thin strips. Warpaint. He couldn't remember where he'd gotten the idea. Perhaps from his old life. At times, the past would present itself in quick visions, flashes of something he wasn't sure was dream or memory. Sometimes smells would do that, the scent of prey with its hint of musk or flowers. The fruity smell of a woman's hair, and even once when he'd split the stomach of an obese man with a belly full of food, a picture flashed of him as a boy, playing with other children and eating phallic-shaped meat near a fire—food he hadn't had in 20 years. That is, if the food was a memory and not a dream.

He headed toward the jet. Once there, he planned to inspect it closer. He no longer feared the confrontation of others. He would kill them on sight or die trying.

Chapter 24

With their father's weak gait, the boys caught up to him quickly. Noah pointed toward Adam up ahead, who was slowly approaching the jet.

The three brothers crouched, delaying their attack for fear of those in the jet. They would let their father face the flashing weapon, perhaps killing him so they didn't have to.

They watched him peek through the windows, run his hands alongside the giant thing.

Through the jet's windows, Adam could see two bodies inside. There was no telling how old they were. Bringing spoiled meat back home would deepen the hole he'd found himself in. If he was even allowed home again.

After circling the jet, he could find no way in. He speculated on where the door might be but was confused on how to open it. Then he saw Abraham's corpse. The condition of his son's body threatened to strike fear into Adam, but he denied it. He would never again entertain anything other than courage. Fear, like his left eye, was no longer a part of him.

The jet was only a short stop to see if there were others, and from what he'd seen through the windows, there weren't. He had scared them earlier. They'd ran screaming, fearing for their lives. Adam smiled at the thought.

He took note of the direction they had headed. Toward Heaven. The forbidden zone. If Adam went there, it would be the first time any of them had. Heaven was a place meant only for God, and the dead. He often speculated on why it was off limits. Was it because the home held secrets? Or was it a test to see if those who dare penetrate its walls truly carried the strength worthy of experiencing the bliss within?

Following the prey's footsteps along the shore was too simple. This was no hunt. No stirring chill in his belly anticipating the moment he'd face the adversary. With the footprints, it was as easy as snatching the toddlers God sometimes offered. The meat was a delicacy, but the thrill absent.

The boys let their father get some distance between them before they crept from the jungle. They agreed that attacking him now, so near the jet, could prove to be a bad idea. So, they followed him for several minutes, realizing he was following a set of tracks. Tracks that stuck to the shore, getting uncomfortably close to the forbidden zone.

If Adam turned now, he would see them, and eventually he *would* turn. He would not continue past the bend. All of them, at one point, had come to the bend, only to lay eyes on God's domain. But not one dare approach it. Once, when Abraham wandered too close, a loud noise echoed through the jungle, scaring them back. They deemed it a warning. The books they'd read, and the lessons given by their mother also gave warnings that man could not survive God's presence, and to even consider it would end in death.

Adam drew closer to the bend. He found himself slowing, blaming his gimped leg, though knowing deep down that while he no longer carried the fear of man, the fear of God still ran through him.

As he rounded the bend, he was awestruck by the beauty of the structure—its walls towering anything he'd ever seen, except for those from his visions. His dreams. His memories. Part of him longed to die right that moment, to find himself within those walls, feasting with God and the scrumptious meat reserved only for those who have passed on.

Just as he had assumed, the footprints had made their way here, not only toward the building but directly into it.

Adam knelt and closed his eyes, then shouted. "Forgive me God, but those you offered have run this way. I come only to receive them."

The prayer was half true. As Adam stepped forward, he knew he would feel the pull of entrance, and that if he did not drop dead by the time he reached the door, he would enter and meet God face to face.

He had done it. He had turned the bend.

"We shouldn't go," Noah said.

"He deserves to die," Abel's lip snarled.

Cain nodded. "Abel is right. And God must know this. Adam walks on God's land this moment, undeserving."

"But how are we deserving?"

"We weren't before, but because of what Adam has done to Mother, we are only here to punish, to do what God wants done."

Noah contemplated his brother's words. They were older, wiser. They taught him how to hunt and gut. And the stories they told deep into the night opened Noah's mind. Who was he to question them now?

Noah nodded, and was the first to run forward, toward Heaven.

The boys sprinted, eager to catch their father before he got too close to God's house, but when they finally reached the bend, bringing God's domain into view, Adam was already approaching the door, creeping, spear out in front of him.

Chapter 25

The cell door opened. It was Simon. He pointed the gun at Caleb. Kevin hadn't noticed before, but Simon's face didn't hold the same contempt the doctor's did. In fact, while the doctor seemed to enjoy the grief he'd put them through, Simon's demeanor was different. There was almost a sadness in his eyes, as though everything he did was not by his hand but someone else's, and if he had his way it wouldn't have come to this.

Simon was standing in the large puddle of piss. He kicked a foot out and the urine splashed. Kevin nearly took advantage of the moment by kicking the man's other leg out from under him. But with the gun on Caleb, he couldn't risk it.

"Young man." He kicked out again, splashing more urine, as though it was nothing but paper stuck to his shoe. "I'm moving your parents to another room. If you have to use the bathroom, I'll take you. But I'd appreciate it if you didn't pee on the floor ag—"

A loud bang from the far side of the building echoed through the empty space, startling Simon. He quickly turned. This time, Kevin took advantage of the moment and kicked as hard as he could into the center of Simon's leg. The man's knee snapped backward, and the gun went off, the sound deafening.

Kevin looked at Caleb, looked at his wife. Neither had been hit.

Simon was on the floor, covered in urine. Both Caleb and Kevin jumped on top of him, wrestling the gun out of his hand. Caleb bit the man's hand and clawed at his face. Before long, Kevin had the gun.

A door slammed and the doctor appeared. He looked at Kevin, saw the gun.

Another loud bang that seemed to be coming from the entrance door.

The doctor swung his head toward the door, then ran to the monitor, ignoring Kevin. He looked at the screen. "Dammit! What in God's name is he thinking?"

Kevin came up behind the doctor, looked at the monitor. The screen offered a view of the front of the building, showing a dark-skinned, dreadlocked man fiddling with the door, trying to open it. It was the man he'd seen near the jet.

Without acknowledging Kevin, Dr. Barnard quickly opened a desk drawer and reached inside. Kevin kicked at the drawer. The doctor screamed and pulled back his broken hand, cradling it close to him. The drawer slid back open, and Kevin could see a pistol inside. He grabbed it.

"You don't know what you're messing with, Mr. Kevin. You have no idea."

"And I don't give a shit. Only thing I'm concerned about is getting my family off this island, which you and your lackey are going to help us with."

The doctor spilled a weak laugh. "Like I said...you have no idea."

"How do the two of you get off the island?"

The doctor said nothing, only stared at Kevin.

"Dr. Barnard, we may as well—" Simon started.

"You say a word, and I'll see to it you're feasted upon." The doctor kept his eyes on Kevin.

Vicki grabbed her son and scrambled from the cell, away from Simon.

The noise at the door grew louder.

"You may as well fill us in, Simon. The doctor isn't going anywhere, and neither are you. Vicki take this gun."

While Kevin was handing Vicki the gun, the doctor swung his good fist at Kevin.

The gun went off, and the doctor fell back with a hole in his chest, cracking his head on the floor.

"Kevin!" Vicki gasped.

Kevin couldn't tell if he'd fired the gun on accident or meant to put the pig down, growing tired of the bullshit. If he had to kill everyone here, he would. Right in front of his boy, because this wasn't the creation of more scars, it was survival at all costs, and one step closer to being the dream dad.

He spun toward Simon, pointed the gun. The cowering man backed against the wall, leaving a trail of piss like the slug he was.

"How the fuck do you leave this island?!" Kevin yelled.

"A boat comes. They bring provisions, sometimes workers for repairs or additions." Simon's voice was a fluttering bird's wing caught in a web. "Th...They won't let you leave. If they find you here, they'll kill you. This is a private operation. It goes much higher than you think. Only a handful know what goes on here."

"Which is what exactly?"

"The study of mankind, the tendency for primitive savagery and survival...to watch a tribe build itself, the habits they acquire, the culture they establish."

"Did you plant these people here?"

Simon hesitated, shook his head in disappointment. Kevin wasn't sure if it was disappointment in himself and what he had done, or for merely getting caught doing it.

"Yes. We...twenty years ago we...we started the tribe with a 12-year-old girl, who would be a mother to the rest. Some she gave birth to, others were brought in by us as babies...except Adam. He was eleven. He was to be the father."

"You're abducting children?" Vicki said.

Simon hung his head.

"And creating cannibals...American, English-speaking cannibals. You gave them the means to read and write, yet you feed them human flesh. You were supplying that too, weren't you? You took innocent children and created monsters." Kevin's face curled in disgust. "And now you're their god."

"It was just supposed to be a simple study. The god thing came later. It was unexpected, but I think Dr. Barnard reveled in it, like some morbid motivation to—"

Kevin raised the gun and shot Simon in the head, painting the wall behind him a pulpy red.

"What in God's name are you doing, Kevin?!" Vicki screamed.

"What do you expect me to do?"

"You didn't have to kill him!"

"I'm not letting anyone stop me from getting my son off this fucking island."

"You could have put him in that room."

"He deserved to die. They both did."

The noise at the door continued.

Vicki began to whine, holding Caleb close to her. "We're never getting out of here."

"Yes we are." He looked at the monitors, the clutter of papers.

"You heard what he said. This whole thing is one big secret. And we're loose ends."

"We're getting off the island, and we're going home."

The noise at the door stopped.

Kevin looked at the monitor. The man was gone.

Kevin suddenly became aware of the pain in his shoulder where the spear had stuck him the day before. He looked at his shirt. Fresh blood. "How are your ribs?" he asked Vicki.

"Sore."

"Okay, stay close." Kevin made his way to the door some thirty feet away, the echo of their steps bouncing off the walls.

They stood at the door and listened. Nothing.

"Don't come out until I say." Kevin opened the door, slowly. He stepped out, looked around. No sign of the man. He held up his hand for Vicki and Caleb to stay, but his wife ignored him and stepped through the doorway. It was then that the dreadlocked man revealed himself from around the corner of the building and threw his spear. Out of his periphery, Kevin saw three more figures pour from the jungle to his right.

There was a wet thud, followed by the sudden gasp of air which barely held the rasp of Vicki's voice. Kevin knew before he looked that she'd been hit. Caleb's screams verified it.

Kevin raised the gun and fired, missing the man who now charged—a maddening look in his one wild eye. He seemed to glide across the sand like a black ghost. But a second pull of the trigger sent the ghost to the ground, landing face-first in the sand.

Kevin turned. Vicki lay on the ground, the spear jutting from her throat, pulled by gravity, and stretching wide the hole it'd made. Blood bubbled and roiled like boiling mud.

The others ran toward him. Boys, one of them Caleb's age.

"Caleb! Stay inside!"

But Caleb didn't listen either, he ran to his mother and retrieved the gun clamped in her hand.

Kevin fired his gun and one of the older boy's fell, his thigh bloodied. He fired again, missing. A boy threw his hammer. Kevin managed to dodge it and fired another round. This one landing just beneath the boy's nose, ripping through his teeth and shattering the back of his skull.

Caleb fired at the last of them, the young boy. Fear in his blue eyes. The boy pulled his arm back to throw the spear, and Caleb fired once more, the bullet sailing past his target. Then Kevin fired and the bullet met the boy's stomach. He went down like the dreadlocked man, landing on his face, but snapping his arm in the process.

Caleb dropped to his knees and pulled the spear from his mother's throat, then wrapped his arms around her and cried. Kevin didn't react, didn't shed a tear. Not because he needed to be a rock for his son, but because he was in survival mode, full of rage, as though the island had infected him with the same savagery its inhabitants held. He was breaking.

He grabbed the hammer and ran for the boy he'd shot in the thigh, who was now crawling toward the jungle, dragging his leg. He raised the hammer and screamed as he brought it down. The steel hit bone with a loud crack. He swung again and again, until the skull caved and the hammer sunk, splashing Kevin's face with warm, gelatinous blood.

His breathing was rapid, dog-like. And when he looked at his son through saucer-wide eyes, he knew there were no words that could take any of this back. The scars were legion now. Scars upon scars.

He turned to the jungle, watched it closely, holding the gun in front of him, aiming at the slightest movement, as leaves shifted in the breeze and birds launched from their perches.

"Dad!"

Kevin ran to him.

"What do we do? Mom is..." The broken words morphed into an unintelligible mash of syllables as he began to wail.

"Let's get back inside."

As if on cue, a buzz sounded and the door slammed shut and locked. Unless someone else was inside, the door had to have been set to automatically lock. Something had triggered it. Sensors? Was it programmed? Or perhaps the powers that be locked them out remotely, privy to the falling of their cannibal empire.

Kevin tried turning the knob. He kicked at the door, threw himself against it. It was never going to budge. With the second floor of the building being nearly twenty feet off the ground, there was no way up. A lot of time, planning, and money had gone into the structure. Anyone who didn't belong was never meant to get in, be it the tribe or a stranded and starving family.

He checked the ammo in the guns. His held a single bullet, as did Caleb's. Wasting them on the steel door was a bad idea. He imagined it could take the abuse, the lock bolt being longer than most. There was also concern for running into more of the tribe.

"Now what?" Caleb's voice was filled with panic, his face stuck in a tragedy pose.

Kevin knelt, grabbed his son by the shoulder. "Listen. I'm sorry, Caleb. I'm so sorry. I know you're scared, but we need to keep it together, and we need to be careful. We're getting off this island. I promise. Okay? I promise. Just stay close and keep your eyes open. Tell me if you see anything at all. Movement, an animal, another person. Anything you see, tell me."

He grabbed one of the spears and gave it to Caleb, then grabbed another for himself, leaving the one that had killed Vicki.

Being wary of another attack, watching the jungle closely, he led his son around the entire building, searching for another door or window, perhaps even a secret way in, feeling along the walls, studying the ground. Nothing. The only way in was locked.

Kevin felt more helpless, more frustrated, now than ever, knowing what they might need was on the other side of those walls. They backtracked, checking every area meticulously. He felt like a mouse in a maze looking for the cheese but being denied the reward because of a fucking wall.

He looked at the windows twenty feet up. They may as well have been on the moon. No amount of wishing he could jump that high would do any good. They stared at the building, contemplating.

Another thing to consider was the powers that be. A government agency? Something even higher? They could be on their way. Or they could ignore it all and let the project die, sending someone to torch the building and any evidence inside.

"We're not getting in there," Kevin finally said. "We should head to the jet and eat what little food we have there. Then we'll check the luggage for anything we may have missed."

He meant Carmen's luggage, but Kevin knew mentioning the name would be another unnecessary kick to Caleb's gut.

It was hard to say how heavily the tribe relied on the scientists for food and water. Kevin knew they were fed human flesh, but what of water? Or did they have their own source near their camp? And why hadn't Kevin seen a single fucking piece of fruit? No bananas. No mangos. No coconuts. Trying to consume anything they didn't recognize would be Russian roulette.

Because of the traps, potentially dangerous animals, and being unsure how many of the tribe were still left, Kevin felt it best they head into the jungle as a last resort only, circling it first. From what he could remember, as they were flying toward it, as well as having already explored a large section of the shoreline, the island wasn't that big. He guessed somewhere between 10 to 20 miles from one end to the other.

They trekked the two miles back to the jet with no sign of any tribe member. They had also kept an eye on the sea, wondering if the powers would show. Kevin suddenly recalled what he'd seen on the monitor when viewing the tribe's camp: The shoreline. The tribe's camp was near it, very near it. If they stuck to the shore, they would eventually run straight into it, and Kevin knew there was at least one member left. A woman.

Chapter 26

They took every suitcase and travel bag into the jet and shut the door so they could go through them without the constant paranoia of a flying spear. Other than clothes, they found cologne, perfume, shampoo, an electric razor, a few cameras, a handful of books and comics, pens, and writing pads. But in Carmen's suitcase was a bottle of wine and a letter addressed to Kevin. He folded it and stuck it in his pocket before Caleb saw.

Kevin changed his shirt and tossed the bloodied one aside, then made a bandage and secured it with a strip from another shirt.

"You should wash that out," Caleb said. "It could get infected."

"You're a smart kid...you know that?" But Kevin wasn't going to wash it. That meant turning his back on the jungle, like a deer in a hunter's sights while drinking from a creek.

When they went for the food, it was gone. Every bag empty, every package opened. Kevin wasn't sure who'd eaten it all. Ross? Vicki? Even from the grave they betrayed him.

"Well...you ready to head out?" Kevin asked.

"I'm tired."

Caleb didn't look good. His eyes were swollen and red, his lips dry. He sat slouched, gazing at the cockpit door. Kevin felt weak and knew he must look just as bad as his son. After having not eaten since the restaurant the day before, he was ravenously hungry. Thank God for that little bit of water.

Thank god. Kevin nearly laughed.

"You wanna stay another night in the jet, get some rest?"

Caleb nodded and laid back in the seat, closing his eyes. Kevin watched him, recalling him as a baby and how he and Vicki never had the problems some parents have, their baby up all night, hungry, crying. Caleb was an angel. *Is* an angel.

"We're getting out of here, my son," Kevin whispered too quiet for Caleb to hear. "I promise."

While Caleb slept, Kevin opened the bottle of wine and took a drink. He knew it was a bad idea, dehydrating him even more, but the pull of alcohol under such duress was impossible to stave off.

He opened the letter he'd found in Carmen's luggage and read it. It was a lengthy confession of her love for him—a wordier version of what she'd shouted just before they crashed. Because of Vicki's history with other men, he felt no true guilt. But why do that to Caleb? Risk losing her as a nanny, risk divorce—even though there were plenty of grounds for one. It was a weak decision made by the old him, the old dad who never put his child first. But now...Caleb will always be first. Kevin needed to find him food, even if that meant playing guinea pig to an unidentifiable fruit. If he ever found one. His only hope was the tribe's camp. If there was anything edible on the island it would be there, including water.

Before capping the wine and falling asleep, he drank half the bottle, finding very little escape from the haunting reality they faced, wondering if it wouldn't be better if they just woke up dead.

Chapter 27

Kevin woke thinking of the watch Vicki had bought him on their fifth wedding anniversary. He'd stopped wearing it when he found out about her first affair. She never even noticed.

He was surprised at how bad his head hurt after only a half-bottle of wine. *Fucking dehydrated. It was a stupid move.*

He looked over at Caleb, who lay there with his eyes open. "Caleb?"

"Yeah?"

"Just checking." *Seeing if you're alive.* "Talk to me...tell me what you're thinking."

"I'm thinking about Carmen's homemade cookies."

"The oatmeal raisin ones?"

"No, the peanut butter ones. She used to put brittle in them so they were crunchy."

"Yeah...they were pretty good." Kevin gave it a moment, thinking of what his first meal would be once they were rescued. "When we get off the island, what's the first thing you want to eat?"

"Carmen's peanut butter cookies."

Even if—*no, even when*—they get off the island, Kevin wondered what kind of normalcy his son could return to, if any at all. Would his days consist of merely existing, lying around, wishing his mother and Carmen were alive, no longer capable of having even simple conversations with a blissfully ignorant friend because he'd seen too much?

"Ready to head out?" Kevin stood up, his hollow gut and weak legs begging him not to.

"Too tired."

"Yeah...me too. But we can't sit and rot in this jet. The longer we wait, the longer we go without food. Once we find that camp, there'll be something there for us. You ever had a mango?"

"No."

"They're juicy. Very sweet, like a peach and pineapple mashed together."

Caleb sat up, held his stomach. His eyes looked like they'd aged several years over night. "What does it feel like to starve to death?"

With the most convincing voice he could muster, Kevin said, "I dunno, buddy. But we're never gonna find out."

He could tell by his son's face that optimism did nothing—It was hard to believe you'll stay afloat and unscathed, when you're surrounded by sharks with no sign of land.

To keep his mind off his empty stomach and desert throat, Kevin took the boy outside and taught him to use the gun, going over what he knew about aim and safety. Without the ability to practice firing, it made for a quick lesson.

"You've got one bullet and that's it. You gotta make it count. You're a little guy, so you might want to aim low because that thing will kick. And when it does, your arms will go up, and so will the bullet."

Caleb held the gun out in front of him, aiming at the boy his father had killed with the flare gun. He squinted down the site, aimed low, and pretended to pull the trigger.

Chapter 28

Every quarter mile or so, the two dipped into the jungle, searching for food. What in the hell were the animals eating? Where in the hell were the animals? All they'd seen so far were birds and the boar. It was as though the island was wiped free of things that should be present. The wildlife, the edible vegetation, the sound of howling monkeys.

Caleb shambled through the sand as they walked under the hot sun, barely lifting his feet. His lips were caked with flaking skin, his posture lax.

After reaching what appeared to be the end of the island and keeping right along the shore, Caleb asked if they could rest.

"I'm beat too, kiddo. But the food isn't going to come to us. We have to go and get it."

"But there isn't any food," Caleb whined. "It's just a bunch of leaves and grass."

"The camp, son. It's along this shore somewhere. They've gotta have something."

After only another twenty minutes of kicking sand with lead feet, Kevin spotted the top of what looked like a large, primitive hut through the thinning trees. He instructed Caleb to crouch, as they hid behind the foliage, quietly making their way forward.

As they grew closer to the camp, they could hear the high-pitched tone of what sounded like a girl humming a song. With guns drawn, they stuck to the sand to keep their steps silent, staying low.

Kevin could see a dead campfire and several tall bamboo spikes jutting from the ground like some sort of fence, or an attempt at decor on a sandy front lawn.

Finally, Kevin saw the girl. She sat on the ground within a large circle of stones with her back to them. She couldn't have been more than 9 years old.

They moved silently behind the tall grass and thick brush, peeking through gaps in the leaves until they saw another girl, much younger, sitting in front of the other.

As they moved closer, toward the spikes, there didn't seem to be anyone else, though the hut was large and could house any number of them. Kevin realized they were at a point where it didn't matter. They would either eventually die of starvation or die right now at the hands of the tribe. No other option presented itself other than to confront whatever lived here, survived here.

They crept closer still, and Kevin got a better look at what the girls were doing. The older one had a human head in her lap, removing its teeth by gently tapping them with a hammer. She would hand them to the younger girl, who would count them, then carefully place them in a small pile next to her. When the girl turned the head to reach the molars with the claw end of the hammer, Kevin saw that the face was mostly gone, but he recognized the dark hair, peppered with gray.

Ross!

"What in the fuck are you doing?!" Kevin jumped from his position and ran around the spikes. If anyone was in the hut, they'd heard him.

The youngest girl sat still, her tiny hand full of teeth. But the other girl tossed the head aside and jumped up with the hammer, charging Kevin with a banshee scream. When she reached him, he caught her in the head with the dull end of the spear, knocking her to the ground. The blow stunned her senseless.

"Caleb! Stay there."

The younger girl ran from the circle and into the hut.

Kevin pointed the gun at the hut's entrance, waiting for the flood of cannibals.

A single bullet. A spear. And his will to live, to be a father. It's all he had.

He waited. The flood didn't happen.

The older girl stood, and again she charged. He repeated the same blow ot her head, and she dropped to the sand in an unconscious heap.

"Come here, son."

Caleb ran to his father.

"I'm going in there, watch the girl. If you see anyone else, shoot them. If you see two of them. Run."

Caleb readied his gun.

Slowly, Kevin approached the hut. It was comprised of two very large rooms. He could see just inside the first room, where a woman lay on the ground, the young girl's arms wrapped around her.

"Is anyone else here?" he asked the girl. He didn't expect an answer, but the girl shook her head no. "Where is everyone?"

A shrug of the shoulders.

As Kevin entered the hut, he could tell right away the woman was dead. Her face smeared with dried blood, her skin a pale blue. This was the mother of the tribe. "Who did this to her?"

"Adam." The girl's voice was quiet, timid. She tucked her legs to her chest, protecting herself.

Was the tribe so savage they killed their own? He recalled the scientist's discussion regarding Adam and his outburst at the hut. This must be the aftermath. But why hadn't the other children stayed with her? Did they all rebel with Adam? Kevin figured the dark-skinned man with the dreads was Adam, now dead outside the complex with a hole in his chest.

"How many of you are there?"

The girl didn't answer. She just shut her eyes, burying her face in her mother's breast.

Quickly, Kevin ran to the next room and saw that it was empty. He counted the beds, then counted how many of the tribe he knew for sure were dead. There were six dead, seven beds. The two girls were alive. Adam most likely shared a bed with the mother—Eve, wasn't it? How biblical, the scientists creating their own genesis.

He went back outside and looked around. There was still no sign of a garden or anything nearby that looked edible. He looked to Caleb, whose eyes were filled with terror.

"What is it, Caleb?"

The boy pointed toward the stone circle with a quick side-eyed glance. Kevin looked. Hanging from the tree was Melanie, split from her crotch to her chin, arms missing. Under her was Ross's headless body, as well as Jennifer, her head intact but slick with skull where her scalp should be. Both of them had been skinned.

161

"Oh God." He grabbed Caleb, pulling him close.

A groan behind him. The older girl was stirring. Kevin spotted a rope on the ground and grabbed it. He dragged the girl by the foot through the sand, and by the time she was fully awake, he had her bound to a tree within the stone circle.

She blinked several times, wincing, looked at the rope wrapped tightly around her, then at Kevin. "God will kill you for this."

"Your god is dead."

Chapter 29

The younger girl sat next to her sister, head resting on her shoulder.

"Where's your food?" Neither of the girls would say a word. He'd asked several times—nicely, then with intimidating shouts. They wouldn't budge. He thought of tying the younger girl to the tree as well, but she didn't seem to be a threat, though if it came to it, he wouldn't hesitate.

He searched the hut again, looking under their makeshift beds, tearing into them. The rooms were loaded with literature, notebooks, pencils, paper, crayons, and knick-knacks made from bone, hair, and leathery hide that Kevin assumed was human. There was also a basket of what looked to be jerky. But before temptation struck, before he was even able to smell its gamey scent, he carried the basket to the water and tossed it in the sea. Then wondered if that was a rash decision and maybe he should have considered asking Caleb first on whether or not he wanted to partake in the abominable act of eating human flesh.

No. I did the right thing. Why tempt him?

But he could die.

While near the water, he called his son down, and the two washed the grime and blood from their skin. The allure to drink from the sea was nearly unbearable, and Kevin made sure to remind his son the danger in doing so.

"Not even just a little, Dad?" Caleb's mouth was filled with strings of chalk-white saliva, like spokes on a bicycle tire, his lips two dirt roads having never seen rain.

Kevin nearly broke down and told his son to go ahead, drink all you want. He screamed and punched the water, wishing it could somehow break on impact, cracking the entire world in half. With clenched teeth, he ran back toward the camp, Caleb following close behind.

"Where the fuck is your water?" he yelled.

Nothing but dirty looks from the two girls.

"Tell me how you drink or I'll...I'll..."

Then Kevin saw the youngest girl give a quick glance toward the back of the hut. He ran to investigate and found a well-trodden path that had seen years of traffic. He and Caleb followed the short trail, where it led to a small watering hole that looked to be manmade, as the border of the hole was covered in broken concrete. Kevin guessed the hole was either filled naturally with rain or by the scientists themselves.

He studied the vegetation around the hole. More of the same. The scientists had to have stripped the land of anything edible. Afterall, how can you create cannibals when you've given them alternative means of nutrition?

After bloating themselves with water, Kevin had his son rest in the hut, while he brought Eve's body out and buried her in the sand. He dug a shallow grave using his hands and the claw-hammer. The grave was more to keep the inevitable stench at bay than out of respect, though he did have sympathy for her. She'd been kidnapped and brought to a desolate place, brainwashed, and used as a host for birthing more cannibals for the manmade tribe. He wondered how much of the real her had still remained after all these years of becoming someone else.

Sitting side by side, the two girls watched with sealed mouths, emotionless. Kevin wondered if the youngest girl even understood death. Had either of them experienced loss before? Perhaps the scientists culled members they deemed a hindrance to their project. And if they had experienced loss, did they even practice burial, or did they eat their dead?

After asking the children once again where food could be found, Kevin grew tired of their silence, tired of being preoccupied with food, and spent the rest of the day digging shallow graves for the Robertsons. He made sure Caleb was still asleep before getting Melanie down from the tree and dragging the family to their graves.

Next, Kevin cleared the entire camp of anything that resembled a body part: sinew, teeth, hair, bones, skin that hung from branches within the circle, and a reeking boar's head that'd spent too much time in the sun. He threw it all into the sea, then took the planted sticks and spelled S.O.S. in giant letters in the sand.

Using the tribe's wood and Vicki's lighter, Kevin made a fire just outside the circle. It seemed a waste. It wasn't cold, and there was nothing to cook, but the fire felt right, the only thing right since they'd gotten on the jet.

Kevin was sitting in the sand, facing the sea, when Caleb stumbled from the hut, arms wrapped around himself. "Did you find any food?"

Kevin shook his head. He felt shame, like he could have done better, like there should have been an entire meal waiting for his boy when he woke.

Caleb joined him in the sand and watched the sun disappear. The sky bled pink and orange, the trees turned to black silhouettes, and the water tickled the sand with quiet ripples.

Kevin looked at the older girl, shifting, struggling to get comfortable. And the younger girl, glaring back at him.

The smoke from the fire reminded him of S'mores. Caleb's favorite. Even more than ice cream. They'd had a fire in their backyard once, listening to the crickets, breathing summer air filled with freshly-cut grass—one of not enough memories made. They were still both so young, decades ahead of them, a second chance at being a *real* father. Yet here they were, starving to death. And he had promised that wouldn't happen, that they would survive.

For God's sake, if you can't trust your father, who can you trust?

With a stomach full of cobweb and a head filled with home, Kevin grabbed the hammer, then made his way into the circle of stones.

Other Books by Chad Lutzke

Of Foster Homes and Flies

Stirring the Sheets

Wallflower

Out Behind the Barn (co-written with John Boden)

Skullface Boy

The Pale White

The Same Deep Water as You

Slow Burn on Riverside

The Neon Owl: Book 1 - When the Shit Hits the Van

Wormwood (co-written with Tim Meyer)

Bloodletter: The Hemato Pages Book 1 (written as C.E. Lutzke)

Spicy Constellation & other Recipes (collection)

Night as a Catalyst (collection)

To join my VIP reader list and be included in all future giveaways, visit www.chadlutzke.com

To become a patron and receive exclusive content, visit

www.patreon.com/ChadLutzke

Chad has written for Famous Monsters of Filmland, Rue Morgue, Cemetery Dance, and Scream magazine. His short fiction can be found in several dozen magazines and anthologies, and some of his books include: OF FOSTER HOMES & FLIES, STIRRING THE SHEETS, THE PALE WHITE, SKULLFACE BOY, THE SAME DEEP WATER AS YOU, and THE NEON OWL. Lutzke's work has been praised by authors Jack Ketchum, Richard Chizmar, Joe R. Lansdale, Stephen Graham Jones, Tim Waggoner and his own mother. He can be found lurking the internet at www.chadlutzke.com

I Believe in Gratitude

Thank you to the following people who helped in some way with the creation of this book: My wife who argued with me about the end and gave valuable feedback, Jeremy Wagner, Bob Ford, Max Stark, Jeremy Hepler and his wife. Brad Proctor, Ross Jeffery, Beth Lee, Holly Rae Garcia, Karen Boden, and Christopher O'Halloran for beta reading. Blaine Cook for permission to use The Accused lyrics. A giant-sized thank you to my wonderful patrons: Beth Lee, Mike Perez, Shannon Bradner, Crystal Staley, Richard Martin, Blake Devours, Joe Mynhardt (Crystal Lake Publishing), Janine Pipe, Sargeras Bolg, Phillip Frangules, Varian Ross, Vitina Molgaard, Connie Bracke, Holly Rae Garcia, Janelle Janson, Stewie, Levi Walls, Mathieu Fortin, Karen Moore, Lee-ann Oleski, Stephanie Briggs, Dirk Gard, Rachel, Alyssa Manning, Jason White, Mary Kiefel, Danielle Milton, Jerri Nall, Melissa Potter, Robert Dabicci, Kimberly Napolitano, John Questore, Jamie Goecker, Wayne Fenlon, Shannan Ross, Night

Worms (Sadie Hartmann and Ashley Saywers), Liane Abe, George "Book Monster" Ranson, Tim (Captain Trips), Steve Gracin, Justin G, Glenda Magner, Alfie, Glen Krisch, Daniel Jervelius, Jon Cowles, Cyndie Randall, Sheila Porter, Kristyn Kasper, Hunter Shea, and Steve Barnard.

Printed in Great Britain
by Amazon

15860311R00099